The Unseen Thread

Kimber Guise

ISBN: 979-8-9994794-0-2

Cover design by Kimber Guise

*Printed in United States

Published by Guise Publishing House

First Edition

This is a work of fiction.

Names, characters, businesses, places, events, locales, and incidents are either the products of the author's imagination or used in a fictitious manner. Any resemblance to actual persons, living or dead, or actual events is purely coincidental.

Table of Contents

Chapter One:
Dreams aren't real, are they?

She didn't sleep that night.

Back in her bunk, Haylee kept the journal she had found in the cabin by her nightstand, unable to stop staring at it.

When she finally drifted off, she dreamed—not in fragments, but in scenes that felt like memories.

She stood in the woods near the cabin. The moon was full. Aggie was there, standing at the edge of a circle carved into the ground, her hands lifted, chanting something Haylee couldn't understand. Firelight flickered in the trees.

Across the circle stood a man. Maybe Elliot.

He didn't seem fully human—at least not in the dream. His eyes glowed faintly gold, and behind him, the air shimmered like a curtain lifting in the wind. Shapes moved in the shadows—tall, lean, and watching. Not animals. Not people.

Aggie's voice rose, and the man stepped forward, hand outstretched. "You must never cross alone," he said, looking past Aggie—at her.

Haylee woke with a start, breath shallow and heart pounding. The smell of fire lingered. And on her windowsill, the frost had formed into the same symbol from the cabin—etched in condensation.

The next morning, she didn't tell her dad. Not yet.

Instead, she put the journal into the trunk with the others for safekeeping.

She sat in front of it, palms resting on the lid, eyes closed. She focused— not sure what she expected, only that the strange energy she'd felt in the cabin was stronger here. Alive.

1

Whispers stirred. Then images. Not dreams—something deeper.

A woman's hands (Aggie's?) weaving herbs through iron wire. A voice chanting in rhythm with a heartbeat. Symbols drawn in ash. A locked doorway carved into stone, flickering between planes—seen only when the blood was awake.

Haylee opened her eyes. Her fingers were warm—and when she looked down, small arcs of heat shimmered from her skin. The metal on the trunk's lock was melting slightly.

She scrambled back, gasping, clutching her hands.

She wasn't imagining it.

She was changing.

Later, in the journal, she found another clue—an entry she hadn't noticed before:

"Elliot is a gatekeeper. Not of heaven or hell, but the space between—the Veil. He is not bound by time. He finds the gifted and awakens what lies dormant. If Haylee finds him before the Veil thins, she may not yet be prepared."

She touched the words, and something clicked into place.

A current running through her bones.

She was being prepared. For what, she didn't yet know. But Elliot… Elliot was waiting.

And the Veil?

It was already beginning to thin.

Bella scratched at the bed. There was a low hum coming from underneath. The trunk. It was calling to her. Bella could feel it. She began to growl.

Haylee had never heard her do that before. It was unsettling.

"Bella, come away from there," she said gently. But as she tried to pick her up, Bella scratched Haylee's arm.

Later that afternoon

Haylee sat in her RV, looking out at the mountains as the sun began to set. A gentle peace settled over her—a quiet assurance that she was exactly where she was meant to be. There was no need to rush forward into the unknown anymore. The future would arrive in its own time. And when it did, Haylee would be ready.

Her phone buzzed, breaking the stillness. It was a text from Jake.

"You're still running away from yourself, aren't you? This little escape is just temporary. You'll come crawling back when you realize you can't do it on your own."

Haylee stared at the message, her grip tightening around the phone. For a moment, doubt crept in like a whisper. But then she remembered Zoe's words. She remembered the strength she had uncovered on this journey. And most of all, she remembered the woman she was becoming.

With a steady breath, she deleted the message.

Not this time, Jake.

She turned off her phone and opened her journal, ready to reflect.

November 28, 2024
I don't know what the future holds, but for the first time in a long time, I feel ready to face it. The road has given me everything I needed—strength, clarity, and a deeper understanding of who I am. Maybe I don't need to figure out everything all at once. Maybe I just need to keep going, trusting that I'll know what to do when the time comes. Whatever happens, I'll be ready.

Haylee closed the journal and leaned back. The stars were just beginning to shine, and above her, the night stretched wide and open. The future was waiting—and she was finally ready to meet it.

Where the road pauses

The next few days passed in a blur of exploration and drives. Haylee wandered through quiet towns, stopping at local shops and scenic overlooks, but no matter where she went, she found herself drifting back to the same café. And each time, Sam was there—offering not just coffee, but conversation that felt grounding in a way she hadn't expected.

Their talks moved easily from playful banter about road life to thoughtful reflections on freedom, purpose, and love. Haylee surprised herself with how much she opened up. She spoke about her childhood, her aunt, and even Jake —past pains she rarely voiced. Sam listened. He didn't interrupt or rush to fix things. He just held space.

One afternoon, after she'd spent the morning writing an article at the café, Sam slid into the seat across from her.

"You said you were figuring things out, right?" he asked, his voice casual but edged with sincerity.

"Yeah," Haylee said, setting her pen down. "That's been the goal."

Sam looked down briefly, then met her gaze. "I've been thinking... I think it's a little easier to figure things out when you're not trying to do it alone."

She was taken aback by the depth of his words. She'd worked so hard to stand on her own, to carve out her independence. She hadn't realized how lonely that stance could feel.

"I'm not saying you need anyone to be whole," Sam added. "But sometimes, someone else helps you see things more clearly. And I think you're already pretty amazing."

A warmth bloomed in her chest. She wasn't sure if it was the words or the way he said them—gently, without expectation—but something inside her softened.

She didn't need to have it all figured out. Maybe, just maybe, being present and open to the unexpected was enough.

Chapter Two:
The Space between Us

Haylee was careful. She didn't want to rush into something she wasn't ready for. But as she and Sam spent more time together, her perspective began to shift.

Sam was patient. He took things slow. He never pressured her for more than she was willing to give—and that alone made her feel safe in his presence.

The days that followed felt like a gentle rhythm—one step forward, one pause to breathe. Haylee explored winding roads through small towns and vast open stretches of land, but her mornings now had a pattern. She returned to the café not just for the coffee, but for Sam. The quiet anticipation she felt as she pulled into the lot had nothing to do with breakfast anymore.

Their conversations deepened, layered with trust. Sam had a way of making her feel seen, even when her words faltered. He asked about her day. He listened without interrupting. He never pushed her to open up—but somehow, she always did.

Still, beneath her growing comfort, something lingered: tension. Not from him, but within herself. Haylee had fought hard to become independent. She'd left everything behind—her job, her house, her old life—to reclaim her sense of self. Now, for the first time in months, she wondered: could she open her heart again?

Was she truly ready to share the pieces she'd only just begun to piece back together?

The answer wasn't as clear as she hoped.

One afternoon, after polishing an article on her laptop, Sam suggested they take a walk by the lake just outside of town. The late sun painted the water in shades of pink and orange. The air was warm and still.

It was the kind of moment she used to dream about—quiet, simple, shared with someone who understood how to just be.

They walked side by side along the gravel path, Josie sniffing happily at every new scent.

Sam broke the silence first. "You've been quiet lately," he said gently.

Haylee glanced at the water. "I've been thinking. About… what this is. Between us."

Sam said nothing at first. He just waited, patient as ever, giving her space to find the words.

"I wasn't planning on any of this," she said quietly. "Not meeting you. Not… feeling this way. Not anytime soon."

She paused, exhaling slowly.

"I left to find myself, Sam. I let go of everything so I could breathe. Be alone. Figure out who I was without all the noise."

He nodded, his gaze steady. "I get that. You've been rebuilding. Learning. Unlearning. And you've done a hell of a job at it. But you don't have to do it all alone anymore."

"I know," she said, her voice barely above a whisper. "But I'm scared. Scared of getting lost again. Of giving up control. Of letting someone in."

"You don't have to let anyone in until you're ready," Sam said gently. "And I'm okay with that. I'm not asking you to change or rush. I'm just here—if you want me to be."

She turned to look at him then, really look. His presence wasn't a demand. It was an offering.

"I've been so afraid," she whispered. "Afraid of losing myself again."

"You won't," Sam said, without hesitation. "You've come too far for that. And I'm not here to take anything from you. I just want to walk alongside you, however long you'll let me."

Haylee's chest ached in that beautiful, terrifying way vulnerability often does.

"I don't know what comes next," she admitted, "but I think I'm okay with that. And I think… I want to see where this goes. With you."

Sam's smile was slow, genuine. "We'll take it one day at a time. No pressure. Just you and me."

Haylee returned the smile, feeling something inside her loosen—a quiet joy, cautious but real.

Just then, Josie ran past them, splashing in the shallows, soaking herself and shaking wildly.

Haylee laughed. "Josie!"

Sam grinned. "I think she approves."

"Well," Haylee said, brushing water from her jeans, "on that note, we should probably get cleaned up."

They walked back together in the fading light, the air filled with the sound of distant crickets and something else—possibility.

The next few days passed with a quiet sense of anticipation. Haylee and Sam spent more time together—sometimes walking, sometimes simply sitting at the café, talking about everything and nothing. There was a natural ease to their connection, something she hadn't felt in years. It wasn't about grand gestures or sweeping declarations; it was about the small, everyday moments that made her feel seen, understood, and valued.

9

But even as she allowed herself to grow closer to Sam, Haylee couldn't help but wonder: was this the beginning of something new? Or was it just another fleeting chapter in her journey?

Chapter Three:
The Heart of the Road

As the days turned into weeks, Haylee began to settle into something that resembled balance. Her mornings were filled with journaling, cleaning Bertha, playing with Josie and Bella, and making the occasional supply run into town. Her afternoons often found her back at the lake, sitting with Sam.

It was an easy routine—simple, nourishing, and exactly what she hadn't realized she'd been needing.

But even as she embraced the peace of it, questions stirred beneath the surface. What did this mean for her journey? For her freedom? For the life she had fought so hard to build on her own terms?

One evening, after a quiet dinner at the café, Haylee and Sam took their usual walk to the lake. The air was crisp, and the sky glowed orange as the sun dipped low over the water. Everything about the moment felt aligned—the quiet, the calm, the closeness.

Josie was nosing around the reeds when she let out a sharp yelp. Haylee and Sam jumped up, thinking she'd been stung. But then, out waddled a skunk.

"Oh no…" Haylee groaned. Josie had been sprayed.

The stench hit them almost immediately.

"Aw, Josie, you poor thing," Sam said, half-laughing, half-choking.

"What am I going to do? I can't let her in the RV like this," Haylee exclaimed, waving a hand in front of her face.

"I've got some tomato sauce at the café," Sam offered. "We used it when Mike's pig got sprayed last year. It worked. Mostly. The pig just smelled like spaghetti for a week."

Haylee laughed in spite of herself. "Desperate times, I guess."

She grabbed a towel from Bertha, and they all walked back to the café. Bella, smelling the offense from inside the RV, bolted out through the open window and ran off indignantly.

Josie, oblivious, trotted along like nothing happened. Sam and Haylee did their best to stay upwind.

As they bathed Josie in the tomato sauce, Haylee chuckled.

"What?" Sam asked, trying not to gag.

"This is just… oddly sweet," she said. "It would make a great addition to my YouTube channel."

She wiped off her hands and reached for her phone, which had been on silent. A new message had come through.

Unknown number:
"You really should be more careful who you hang around."

Haylee froze.

Sam noticed her face change. "What is it?"

She hesitated. "It's another text. From the same unknown number. I've been getting them for months. They always mention Aggie—or me."

Sam's expression darkened. "What did this one say?"

She showed him.

"You really should be more careful who you hang around."

Sam's jaw clenched. "Someone's watching you. And you didn't think to tell me this sooner?"

"It's been a while since the last one," she said quickly, though she knew it wasn't completely true. "And… there's something else."

His brow furrowed. "What?"

"Someone left a note on Bertha's windshield a while back."

"Haylee, that's serious. Did you report it?"

"No. I told my dad. He said he'd look into it from his end. I didn't think to go to the police…"

Sam was silent for a moment. Then his voice softened—but it was firm. "You should stay with me. I've got a spare room. You, Josie, and Bella are more than welcome. Just park Bertha behind the café. I'd feel better knowing you're safe."

She opened her mouth to protest, but stopped. The concern in his eyes said everything.

No one had ever worried about her like this. It felt… nice.

She nodded. "Just for a night or two."

Sam smiled with relief. "Good."

As they cleaned up the last of the tomato-soaked mess, Haylee snapped a selfie with Sam and Josie. The title came to her instantly: *"Josie vs. Skunk."*

It might not have been part of the plan—but it was part of the story.

Unpacking More Than Bags

After Josie got cleaned off, Sam helped Haylee pack a few things. Bella was not fond of leaving her cozy spot in the sink, but she didn't fight Haylee much.

"It's just for a night or two, Bella."

Bella yawned in acceptance, and they made their way to Sam's apartment.

"It's not much, but it has everything I need," Sam said, smiling like a kid showing off his favorite toy.

He had a small two-bedroom apartment just off the side of the café. It was decorated exactly how you'd expect a single guy's place to be: big-screen TV, PS4 with a cabinet full of video games, a futon in the living room, a small kitchenette with a microwave and fridge, and almost no silverware. The spare room had a twin bed and a single window. Sam's room had a king-size bed and a bathroom—with a tub.

Haylee hadn't realized how much she missed soaking in a warm bath. Showers in Bertha were fine, but a bath? That was a luxury.

"Mind if I soak in the tub?" she asked shyly.

"No, go right ahead. I'll take Josie for a walk—help her dry off a bit more." Sam blushed, avoiding her eyes as he turned to leave.

Haylee grabbed her overnight bag and stepped into the bathroom. It was surprisingly clean—not what she expected from a guy living alone. But her mind was on the tub. She filled it with steaming water, added a touch of body wash, and slowly sank in. The heat eased the tension from her muscles. It felt like the stress of the last few days was melting away.

Outside, Sam checked on Bertha, still parked behind the café. He couldn't shake the question circling in his mind: Who would send texts to scare someone like that? What was their motive?

As he walked past the RV, something caught his eye—a figure near the side. Footprints in the dirt. Human, not animal. His own and Josie's left double prints. These stood alone.

When he reached the front, there it was—another note on the windshield:

"Haylee, you aren't fooling anyone. If you wanted to play house, you should've just said so."

He looked around, but the figure had vanished. No more footprints. Nothing. It was as if they'd disappeared into thin air.

Sam ran back to the apartment.

He stepped inside just as Haylee emerged from the bathroom, towel wrapped around her. She blushed. Sam looked away, muttering something and retreating to the living room.

Haylee dressed quickly and joined him. "Is everything alright at the RV?" she asked, combing out her wet hair.

"Uh, well… I don't really know how to say this," he began, pacing.

"What? Just tell me," she urged.

"I saw someone. A figure. But when I got there, they were gone. No footprints leading away. And they left a note."

He handed it to her.

Her breath caught as she read it. "Oh god. What now?"

"I really think we should report this."

"You may be right. I'm sorry for dragging you into this." She sank down beside him on the futon.

"Don't say that. I chose to be here. I want to help figure out who's doing this."

"I'll text my dad. Let him know where I am—and see if he has any updates."

"What does he have to do with this?"

"I don't know. But whoever this is—they know things. About my family. Maybe even more than I do."

Sam nodded grimly. "I'm really glad you're here. In the morning, we're going to the police."

"Let me talk to my dad first, okay?"

"Haylee, I don't think we should—"

"I know. Just… let me hear what he has to say first. Then we go."

Later that night, Josie stretched across the futon while Bella curled on a pillow beside Haylee in the spare room. Sam didn't sleep much. He checked the locks—twice. And each time he peeked in on Haylee, he smiled softly.

She snored just a little when she slept on her back.

It was kind of cute.

Chapter Four:
Through Shadows and Footsteps

Haylee woke to the sharp beep of a truck backing up. For a split second, she forgot where she was.

The room was dim, quiet. Bella snoozed beside her on the pillow. Josie was curled at the foot of the bed. Haylee blinked up at the ceiling, then let the soft scent of coffee pull her memory back into place.

Sam's apartment.

Right.

She pulled on her robe and shuffled down the hallway. Josie perked up and padded after her. As she turned the corner, she found Sam pouring coffee into a travel mug.

"Morning," he said, voice warm and soft. "How'd you sleep?"

Haylee smiled faintly. "Better than I expected. I forgot how much my back hated the RV mattress."

Sam held out the mug. "It's just instant. I usually get the good stuff at the café."

She accepted it gratefully. "Thanks. How about you? Did you sleep okay?"

"I passed out like usual," he lied, not wanting her to know how many times he'd checked the windows.

Haylee glanced at her phone. "I texted my dad last night. Still no response. I'll let you know when I hear from him."

She grabbed Josie's leash. "I should take her out and check on Bertha."

"Here," Sam said, fishing his keyring from the counter. "Take my key. Hang out here whenever. No rush."

She opened her mouth to reply, but her phone buzzed. Both of them froze.

It was a message from her dad:
"Coming soon. We'll talk in person. Not over text."

"That sounds serious," Sam muttered.

"Yeah. He's… cryptic. I haven't actually spoken to him since he left a month ago."

Sam walked her out, and then stepped into the café kitchen. Mike was already prepping the lunch special: pulled pork sandwiches with homemade potato salad.

"Hey, is it cool if Haylee parks her RV behind the café for a few days?" Sam asked, sliding on his apron.

Mike shrugged. "Yeah, just not forever. I don't want folks thinking this is a campground."

"She's staying at my place for a bit. Didn't feel right leaving the RV unattended."

"Fair. Just make sure there's no trash left behind. Or it's your ass."

"Yes, sir." Sam gave a mock salute.

Meanwhile, Haylee walked Josie around Bertha. Something shiny caught her eye beneath the RV. She bent down.

A small, round tag.

Her heart sank.

It looked like a tracker.

That's how they knew where she was.

There was no ID number. Nothing to trace it by sight. But she took a photo and sent it to her dad. Then she pocketed it—she'd take it to the police later.

She checked Bertha's door. The lock was intact. Inside, everything looked undisturbed. Still, her nerves itched.

Haylee grabbed a journal, then she and Josie returned to Sam's apartment. Bella was perched on the kitchen counter, gazing out the window. Josie jumped up on the futon like she belonged there.

Maybe they both needed a break from Bertha, too.

Haylee sat at the counter and opened her journal.

These last few weeks with Sam have been good. Safe. I'm trying not to overthink it. He's kind, calm, and doesn't ask for anything from me. After the texts and the note, I told him everything. I think he already sensed something was off anyway.

He insisted I stay here for a few days. Offered the spare room. Bella approved.

The tub did too.

Sam wants me to go to the police. Especially after what happened last night. He said he saw a figure near Bertha. Human footprints. Then another note on the windshield. But no trace of where the person went.

Vanished.

I'm taking the tracker I found this morning to the police. Maybe they can trace it.

I haven't told Dad I'm staying here. I'm not sure how he'd react. Probably tell me to come home. But this is home—for now. And I'm handling it.

The Circle Grows

Haylee walked to the café and told Sam about the tracking device she found. He reiterated what he'd said before—she needed to go to the police. Just then, Mike emerged from his office.

"What's this now?" he asked.

Sam handed him the device. "Haylee found it under her RV this morning."

Mike examined it for a moment. "I have a buddy at the police station—ask for Detective Riles. If he can't figure it out, he'll know someone who can," he said, handing it back to Sam.

"Thanks, Mike," Sam replied, wiping the device with a napkin before passing it to Haylee. "Put that somewhere safe until we can bring it in tomorrow."

"We?" Haylee asked, trying not to sound defensive.

"Well, yeah. I figured I'd go with you—since I saw the figure and found the second note."

She nodded. "Okay."

Haylee took a seat in a booth by the window and opened her journal.

I'm really glad I'm staying with Sam right now. His boss Mike knows someone at the police station—a detective. Hopefully he can trace the tracking device and stop whoever is behind this.

Dad is coming back for a visit soon. I just wish he'd be honest about what he knows. I'm going to ask him to speak with the detective too.

Just then, a crash of pans clanged to the floor and startled Haylee. Sam popped out of the kitchen window.

"Sorry about that!" he called, waving sheepishly.

She laughed softly. Sam is a good guy… right?

Haylee spent a few more hours at the café, checking emails and her YouTube channel. Her latest video of Josie and Sam covered in tomato sauce had racked up 14k views. The comments were full of laughing emojis and questions about Sam.

Eventually, she headed back to Sam's apartment and decided to take advantage of the bath again. Josie curled up on the bed in the spare room while Bella perched on the futon, watching the world outside.

Haylee was just about to step into the tub when a sharp knock at the front door made her jump.

Her heart pounded. She clutched the towel tighter. Should she answer? It wasn't her place.

She grabbed her phone and dialed Sam.

"Sam," she whispered. "Someone just knocked on the door."

"What? Where are you? Are they still there?"

"I'm in your bathroom. I didn't look. I was just about to get in the tub."

"I'm coming now. Lock the bathroom door and don't move."

Sam quickly told Mike, and they both left the café—it was empty anyway.

But Sam had forgotten something. He'd given Haylee his keys. When they arrived, he had no choice but to kick the door in.

"Sorry, Mike—I'll replace it," Sam muttered.

"Don't worry about it right now," Mike said.

The sound of the door crashing open made Haylee freeze. She didn't dare call out. Josie barked furiously, then abruptly went silent.

Haylee's heart pounded in her ears. She was about to open the bathroom door when a knock sounded on the other side.

"Haylee? You okay?"

"Yeah. What was that noise?" she called, still wrapped in a towel.

"You've got my keys—I had to kick the door in," he laughed.

Haylee opened the bathroom door just as she realized—Sam wasn't alone.

"Don't worry, I'll take it out of his check," Mike joked.

Startled, Haylee jumped back and hit her head against the doorframe. She now stood gripping her towel while two men tried not to stare. She wasn't modest, but this wasn't the time to bare all.

She blushed. The men respectfully looked away. She slipped past them into the spare room to get dressed.

When she returned, the guys were waiting in the living room.

"You okay?" Mike asked, munching on a bag of chips.

"Yeah," she said, rubbing the back of her head. "Did you see anyone?"

"No. Just like before—one set of footprints to the door, but none leading away," Sam replied.

"Eerie, if you ask me," Mike said, mouth full.

"We're going to the police station now," Sam told him. "I'll be back for the night shift."

"Nah, don't worry about it," Mike said, getting up. "I'll call my buddy and let him know you're on the way."

Chapter Five:
Threads of Truth

Haylee sat on the edge of the futon, Bella curled beside her like a silent guardian. The adrenaline still hummed in her veins, even as the room began to settle into its quiet rhythm again. Sam perched on the arm of the futon, elbows on his knees, eyes fixed on the floor.

"I think this is more than just someone messing with you," he said at last, his voice low and certain.

Haylee nodded slowly. "I do too. It feels... calculated. Like they know what matters to me. Who matters to me."

Sam looked up then—really looked at her. "We'll figure this out. You're not alone in this anymore."

She reached out and took his hand. It was warm, steady, and exactly what she needed in that moment.

Haylee opened her journal again while Sam made coffee.

I used to think that fear was something you outran. That if you kept moving, you could stay ahead of it. But maybe fear isn't something you escape—maybe it's something you learn to live beside, without letting it drive.

I still don't know who is sending the texts or how they know about Aggie. But I do know I'm not running anymore. I have people who care. And I have questions that need answers.

Today, we go to the police. Today, I choose not to disappear into the unknown but to stand inside it—open-eyed.

Let's see where this thread leads.

An hour later, Haylee stood outside the police station, clutching the small plastic sandwich bag in her hand. Inside it sat the tracking device—now sealed, but still pulsing with questions she couldn't answer. Sam stood beside her, hands tucked in his jacket pockets, waiting until she was ready.

"You ready to do this?" he asked quietly.

"No," she admitted. "But I'm doing it anyway."

They walked into the lobby, greeted by the chill of fluorescent lighting and the faint hum of paperwork being shuffled somewhere behind a plexiglass screen.

A receptionist glanced up. "Help you?"

"We're here to see Detective Riles," Sam said. "Mike Everett from the café called ahead."

The woman nodded and buzzed them through a set of secured doors.

Detective Riles was younger than Haylee expected—late forties, maybe—dressed in jeans and a blazer that looked like it lived on the back of his office chair more than on his shoulders. He stood when they entered, offering a firm handshake.

"I hear you've got something to show me," he said, motioning them to sit.

Haylee placed the small plastic sandwich bag on his desk. "I found it under my RV. I've been getting text messages, too. Someone's watching me—and they've left notes."

He opened the bag and studied the device. "Looks like a basic Bluetooth tracker, but this one's modded. We'll have our tech team run it through a scan. Anything else?"

"I saw someone," he said, stirring his coffee absently. "A shadow, moving just past the side of her RV last night. No details, no face. Just a figure. When I got there, they were gone."

"Gone?" Detective Riles repeated.

"Yeah. But here's the weird part—footprints. One set leading up to the RV, but none walking away. Like they just vanished."

Haylee had shivered at the memory. That detail had stuck with her all night.

"Then earlier today, someone knocked on the apartment door. No footprints away again. Just... gone."

Riles raised an eyebrow. "You see them?"

"No," Haylee replied.

"And your name?" he asked Haylee.

"Haylee Hensen."

Something shifted in the detective's expression, but it vanished as quickly as it appeared. He scribbled something into a notepad.

"Let me run this," he said, lifting the bag. "In the meantime, stay somewhere secure. Do not go off the grid. If you receive anything else—texts, notes, anything—bring it to me immediately."

Haylee nodded. "Can I ask... have you heard the name Aggie Hensen before?"

That pause again. Not long enough to be awkward—but long enough to be noticeable.

"You'll hear from me within twenty-four hours." Riles replied, avoiding the question.

Shadows in the Rearview

The late afternoon sun stretched long shadows across the parking lot as Haylee and Sam stepped out of the police station. The air felt heavier now, as if their questions had been acknowledged but not yet answered.

Haylee exhaled slowly, gripping her coat tighter. "Did you see his face when I mentioned Aggie's name?"

Sam nodded. "Yeah. He definitely recognized it. He just didn't want to admit it."

They walked to the truck in silence. Bertha felt far away now—almost like another life, though she was only parked a few blocks over. The tracker still sat heavily in Haylee's thoughts, but it was the look on Detective Riles' face that lingered.

Back at the café, Mike met them with two cups of coffee already waiting. "So?" he asked.

Sam gave him a quick recap while Haylee leaned on the counter, tuning in and out, her mind spinning. She pulled out her phone and typed a quick message to her dad.

Can we talk soon? It's important. I need to know everything about Aggie. No more half-truths.

She stared at the message before hitting send.

Bella weaved between her ankles. Josie let out a low woof from her spot near the door. Haylee looked down at them and realized how much these sweet fur babies—these little constants—were keeping her anchored.

"Hey," Sam said gently. "Want to take a drive? Not far. Just... out of town for a bit?"

Haylee hesitated. But maybe that's what she needed—a little space to think.

Sam tells Haylee about an RV festival someone mentioned in passing at the cafe earlier in the week in a nearby town, a gathering of nomads and wanderers, a melting pot of people from all walks of life, all connected by love for the open road. It was called the **Nomad Junction RV Festival**, and it was held every year in a little-known desert town. This year, it promised workshops on rv/van life, solar power setups, cooking on the road, and even live music and RV-themed art exhibitions.

"Sounds like a blast," Haylee said, excitement bubbling in her chest.

"Let's go check it out."

Sam was already climbing in the passenger seat. The idea of connecting with RVers and hearing their stories intrigued him. They both agreed that the RV world was far more vibrant and diverse than they'd ever imagined, and this was a chance for Sam to get a deeper look into it.

When they pulled into the festival grounds, Haylee's jaw dropped. It was massive - like an RV city in the middle of the desert. Dozens of RVs, vans, and campers were parked in neat rows, colorful tents, flags, and banners were everywhere. The air was thick with the scent of fresh coffee and sizzling food from food trucks. There were people setting up booths, chatting animatedly, and playing acoustic music under a string of twinkling lights.

"This is like RV heaven," Haylee muttered, stepping out of Bertha.

"Yeah, this place is buzzing," Sam said, his eyes scanning the sea of fellow travelers.

Nomad Junction

Their first stop was a Nomadic Life workshop, where a group gathered around a converted school bus. The instructor, a warm and animated woman named Vanessa, was a tiny home design expert who'd turned her short bus into a full-time home.

"Hey! You're new around here, huh?" she greeted. "Welcome! I'm happy to show you some tricks and tips—space is king when you're living in a small space."

Haylee felt right at home. Vanessa showed them how to build fold-out desks, efficiently store food and clothing, and create cozy corners in small spaces.

"You'd be amazed what you can fit in when you think outside the box," Vanessa said, holding up a collapsible sink. "This one's my favorite kitchen hack. Use it only when you need it!"

Haylee's eyes lit up. "That's brilliant. I never knew about those."

Ideas for Bertha swirled in her head—clever storage, more light, tiny comforts. That early inspiration she'd felt when she first started fixing up Bertha came rushing back.

They bounced from event to event. One session covered composting toilets—hilarious, but surprisingly useful. Another was led by a man preparing for survival in a zombie apocalypse. Though dramatic, he had practical advice: outfitting your RV for long-term off-grid living, water purification, solar battery setups, even how to convert fuel tanks to run on compost or food scraps if gas stations shut down.

"Gennies will bring the zombies right to you," he joked. "Silent solar? That's how you stay breathing."

Haylee jotted down a few notes while Sam smirked. "You never know," she teased.

Roadside Connections

As the sun dipped lower, they wandered toward the heart of the festival—a large communal space filled with picnic tables, hammocks, and RVs parked in a circle. A banner read: Evening Potluck – All Are Welcome.

"Potluck!" Haylee exclaimed, her eyes lighting up. "I've missed home-cooked food."

She glanced at Sam. "Sorry."

He laughed. "I know what I'm good at. Chili and cereal."

They grabbed plates and mingled. Sam snuck Josie a piece of pork. Haylee acted like she didn't notice, but smiled. They sat with a group of travelers: a retired couple named Ron and Carol who had been full-timers for five years; Mia, a solo traveler and painter who'd sold everything to hit the road; and Rick and Jenna, a young couple living out of a converted Sprinter van.

"Where are you guys headed next?" Ron asked, biting into cornbread.

Sam and Haylee exchanged a glance. They hadn't talked about that.

"It's still up in the air," Sam replied easily, careful not to imply too much.

"What about you?" Haylee asked, redirecting.

"Grand Canyon," Rick said. "I've been, but Jenna hasn't. It'll be our first official landmark."

"You should try the south rim at sunset," Ron offered. "It's breathtaking. But the north rim's quieter if you want to avoid the crowds."

As Sam stuffed his face with baked beans—some of which escaped onto his shirt—Haylee watched him and smiled. Then she found herself wondering what it would be like to share more of the road with him. Not a whole life. Not yet. But maybe a small stretch. One trip. One shared sunrise.

Sure, she had Josie and Bella, but they didn't talk back. They didn't laugh at her jokes or offer to take the wheel.

Sam caught her gaze and smiled again, oblivious to the bean juice on his face.

"I haven't even been there yet," Haylee said. "The Grand Canyon. I'll keep that in mind—if I... uh, we make it out that way."

Sam's confused look softened into something curious. He didn't push. And she didn't elaborate. Not yet.

Stories swirled around them—tales of flat tires in the Rockies, of impromptu music festivals in Oregon, of random roadside kindness in places too small to find on a map.

"You know what they say," Carol added with a wink, "the road always knows how to surprise you."

Mia leaned in, chuckling. "You guys should meet Henry. He's been documenting weird travel stories and had a run-in with someone who claimed to know *exactly* how to manipulate GPS signals. Said he could make a tracker go completely invisible if he wanted to."

Haylee froze for half a beat before covering it with a sip of lemonade. Sam caught the pause. Neither said anything.

Josie yawned and curled up between them, resting her head on Haylee's knee.

Haylee wasn't worried about whatever tomorrow brought, tonight was about comfort food, campfire stories, and the hush of the desert settling in.

Chapter Six:
Wheels in Motion

Haylee, Bella, and Josie curled together in the bed inside Bertha, wrapped in quiet desert stillness and the muffled sounds of distant acoustic music still echoing from the festival grounds. The warmth of the van and the comfort of her furry companions anchored her. Meanwhile, Sam had stretched out on the pull-out couch, already halfway to snoring. It was a makeshift arrangement— but it felt safe.

They awoke to the rising sun streaking the sky with soft orange and lavender hues. Haylee and Sam joined others at the communal breakfast tables. Pancakes, campfire eggs, and locally brewed coffee filled the air with warmth.

"I could get used to this," Sam said, biting into a pancake smothered in syrup.

Haylee sipped her coffee and smiled. "I already was."

They were mid-bite when Sam's phone buzzed.

He glanced at the screen, then stood abruptly. "It's Mike. He says we need to head back. Now."

Haylee set her cup down. "Did he say why?"

"Just that Detective Riles has something and it's important we come back today."

Haylee nodded, the weight returning quietly to her chest.

They packed up Bertha and pulled out of the festival grounds just after breakfast, the festive colors and laughter fading in the rearview mirror. The road ahead shimmered under the morning light, silent and uncertain.

As they drove, conversation ebbed and flowed.

"Sam," Haylee said, glancing over, "Do you think you'd ever want to go back on the road? Like, really travel?"

He looked thoughtful. "I don't know... maybe. For a bit. Why?"

She hesitated. "I've been thinking. If things keep getting weird—these messages, the tracker—I might not want to stay parked in one place. Maybe keep moving. Just for a while."

Sam nodded slowly. "I've actually been thinking the same thing. A change would be good."

Haylee watched the road stretch out ahead. "Would you come with me? If you could get time off?"

He smiled, soft and sure. "If it meant making sure you, Bella, and Josie stayed safe? I'm in."

The decision wasn't final yet, not fully spoken aloud—but in that moment, they both felt it. A beginning.

The wheels were already in motion.

Chapter Seven:
Signs and Silences

Bertha rolled into the café's parking lot just past noon. Haylee spotted a rugged, dark-colored Jeep Wrangler already parked near the back, its windows reflecting the late-morning sun. Her stomach tightened.

Josie gave a small, alert bark from the passenger seat.

"You go on in," Haylee said, clipping Josie's leash on. "I'll take her for a quick walk. Just need a minute."

Sam nodded and hopped out, "I'll check in with Mike."

Haylee walked Josie along the gravel edge of the lot, letting the silence wrap around them. She didn't want to go in there yet. Not until she felt the air clear again. Josie trotted ahead, tail wagging, nose to the ground, blissfully unaware of the tension around them.

Inside, the café was mostly empty. Mike stood behind the counter, polishing a coffee mug with a towel that had seen better days.

"Mike," Sam greeted him.

"Hey, glad you're back. Riles has been pacing in the office. He says he's got something, but he wouldn't spill until you both were here."

"Any idea what it's about?"

"Nope. But he looks like someone who found the end of a thread and isn't sure if he should pull."

Sam ran a hand through his hair. "Great."

Moments later, the door chimed. Haylee stepped in, Josie at her side. Her eyes met Sam's.

"Ready?"

"Let's hear what he's got."

Mike led them through the café and into the back office, where Detective Riles stood with his hands in his pockets, staring at a printout on the desk.

"Thanks for coming in," Riles said, without looking up. "I think it's time we had a deeper conversation about this tracker—and about Aggie."

The Detective's Thread

Haylee exchanged a glance with Sam, then took the seat across from Riles. Sam stood behind her, arms crossed.

Riles finally looked up, his expression unreadable. "I ran the tracker. It's not something you buy at a big box store. It's military-grade. Whoever planted it had access to high-level equipment—and knew what they were doing."

Haylee's breath caught in her throat. "Military?"

"Or someone who knows someone on the inside," Riles said. "This isn't the kind of tech your average creep gets off eBay."

Sam leaned forward slightly. "So who's got access to that kind of thing?"

Riles tapped the paper on the desk. "That's the thing. I can't trace it to a manufacturer, at least not through official channels. But there was a partial ping —just long enough to trace it to a private account."

Haylee narrowed her eyes. "Whose account?"

Riles hesitated. "It was routed through a private security firm. Based in Arizona. A defunct one. The paper trail's almost nonexistent."

"And you think this has something to do with Aggie?" Haylee asked quietly.

Riles's eyes sharpened. "I think Aggie might have been living more than a nomadic life. And if someone's watching you now, it's likely they watched her then."

Haylee's stomach churned.

Haylee leaned forward, her voice quiet. "Do you think whoever planted the tracker... was also watching Aggie?"

Riles gave a slow nod. "That's my guess. This kind of tech doesn't land in someone's lap by accident. My gut says it wasn't about money or surveillance in the usual sense—it was about something personal. Or maybe something... strange."

"Strange how?" Sam asked, glancing at Haylee.

Riles hesitated. "Let's just say I've seen weirder things swept under the rug in small towns. Sometimes things don't add up in any normal way. This doesn't feel like a stalker. It feels like someone who's been pulling strings for a long time."

Haylee's chest tightened. "Elliot?"

Riles raised an eyebrow. "Elliot?" he echoed, like he was testing the weight of the name. He didn't write it down, didn't repeat it again. Just let it settle. "Someone from Aggie's past?" he asked casually, too casually.

Haylee hesitated. "Maybe. He's... he's shown up in ways that don't make sense. Notes. Warnings. He knew her. I think he knows me, too."

Riles nodded slowly, his gaze sharpening but his tone staying neutral. "I'll keep it in mind. People like that—if they're watching, they usually have a reason. And sometimes that reason's buried deeper than we expect."

He paused, then added, "Wouldn't be surprised if someone that had access to gear like this—especially if they're connected to people or groups that operate... off the books."

"Like supernatural off-the-books?" Sam asked, half-joking.

Riles didn't laugh. "Let's just say there's a reason I drive a Jeep instead of a cruiser. I tend to get handed the cases that don't fit cleanly in files." Sam nodded like he expected that.

"Someone who doesn't want to be found. And someone very good at disappearing." Riles paused, then continued, "You both need to be extremely cautious moving forward. Whoever this is—they're watching more than your location. They're watching your decisions."

Haylee swallowed. "So what do we do?"

"I'll keep digging," Riles said, already gathering his papers. "But I suggest you keep moving. If someone is tracking you, staying in one place just gives them time to close in."

He didn't say goodbye. Just nodded once and left through the back.
Haylee sat there, frozen for a moment.

Sam rested a hand on her shoulder. "Well... looks like the road's calling again."

Chapter Eight:
Where We go from Here

Haylee and Sam stared at each other for a moment. Neither was sure what to say. But as always, Josie knew what to do—she laid her head on Sam's knee and looked up at him, as if to say, "I trust you." Sam rubbed Josie's ear, smiling down at her.

"We should come up with a destination, a plan, and get supplies if we're going on the road," Sam said finally. "I'll fill Mike in on a need-to-know basis. I don't want too many people knowing where we are or where we're headed."

"Will Mike give you time off to travel like that? I don't know how long we'll be gone—or even where we're going. And that's the best part." She grinned.

"Yeah, Mike's cool. He won't mind if I'm gone a while. One time, I went to visit my sister in Washington and ended up breaking down there. Mike told me I always have a job here at the café, no matter how long I'm away. He doesn't expect me to stay forever," Sam said, opening the office door.

"I'll need to tell my dad. He's coming back out here," Haylee said.

"Can you tell your dad very little? I want to keep our circle tight right now, for safety reasons."

"Yeah, I get that. Good call."

"Well, alright then," Sam said, "I guess we need to start a supply list and get packing. I'd like to leave by dawn."

Measured Words

Haylee stared at her phone for a moment, trying to gather her thoughts. What was she supposed to tell her dad? Where they were going? No—not yet. They hadn't even decided. She figured she'd keep it light and just find out when he might be heading her way.

She took a breath and dialed.

"Hey, sweetheart," her dad answered. "You doing okay?"

"Yeah," she said, keeping her tone easy. "Just wanted to check in. When are you thinking about coming back out?"

"End of the month, most likely," he replied. "A few things to wrap up here first."

Haylee felt a small wave of relief. That gave them time.

"Good to know. Just so you're aware, I may hit the road again soon. Nothing serious, just feeling like stretching the wheels again. Might be good for me."

A pause on the line.

"Still staying close to the café?"

"For now. But I'm thinking of exploring a bit. I'll keep in touch."

"Alright," he said. "You've always had a good compass. Just keep your head on straight."

"I will."

They exchanged goodbyes, and Haylee set the phone down slowly. She'd said enough—but not too much. And for now, that was exactly how it needed to be.

Now, it was time to get Bertha ready for whatever came next.

Chapter Nine:
Packing for Possibility

The night before their departure, Haylee and Sam hit the small-town general store. It wasn't exactly a supercenter, but it had the essentials—and a few eccentric surprises. Sam held up a can of SPAM in one hand and a firestarter in the other.

"Survival rations and pyromania," he said. "We're ready for anything."

Haylee chuckled as she dropped packets of dried lentils and trail mix into the cart. "Focus, Sam. We need batteries, bottled water, duct tape, and food."

"You're a woman after my own heart."

A Beach Boys track played faintly from overhead speakers, setting a nostalgic tone. By the time they made it to checkout, their cart looked like a doomsday prepper's shopping spree. The cashier, a woman with silver hair and glittery glasses, raised an eyebrow but said nothing as she scanned their items.

Outside, they loaded up Bertha. Josie wagged her tail while Bella yawned from the window perch.

"You ready?" Haylee asked, wiping her brow.

Sam adjusted his sunglasses. "For anything."

Saying Goodbye

Bertha was parked under the soft glow of morning light behind the café, her shadow stretching long across the gravel. Haylee stood at her side, checking her notes.

Sam emerged from the café with two travel mugs and handed one to her.

"Okay, I've got coffee, and Mike's cool with me heading out for a while," he said.

"What'd he say?" Haylee asked, taking a sip.

"He just raised an eyebrow and said, 'Don't get yourself killed, kid.' Then he gave me this." Sam held up a worn but sturdy travel compass. "Said it's from one of his first road trips."

Haylee smiled. "That's oddly sweet. And very Mike."

Josie barked as Bella jumped onto the dashboard inside Bertha.

"Alright," Haylee said. "Let's hit the road."

The Road Beckons

They pulled out just as the first rays of dawn broke across the sleepy town, turning the quiet streets gold. Haylee took the wheel, Bertha rumbling beneath them. Sam played DJ and teased Josie with a rope toy.

"This playlist has a very retro road-trip vibe," Haylee said, smiling.

"Exactly the point. You can't leave civilization without a little Doobie Brothers."

The windows were cracked, letting in the crisp morning air that swept away any lingering tension.

A couple of hours into the drive, Sam reached over and tapped her hand. "Mind if I take a turn driving?"

Haylee hesitated. She didn't usually let anyone drive Bertha. But Sam had shown nothing but care and respect for her little home-on-wheels.

"Alright," she said, pulling over. "Just… be gentle. She's got her quirks."

"You got it," he grinned.

They switched seats. Sam adjusted the mirrors while Haylee settled into the passenger seat, watching him with amusement.

"You look way too comfortable behind that wheel," she teased.

"Natural talent," he replied.

Bella leapt from the back and attempted to perch on the dashboard, knocking over a container of snacks. Josie barked in alarm, then pounced, trying to rescue the runaway granola bars.

"Chaos gremlins," Sam muttered, swerving slightly as Josie clambered up beside him.

"I think they're just making sure you earn Bertha's trust," Haylee said, laughing.

Later, they pulled off at a scenic turnout—an overlook framed by pine trees and rocky bluffs. Sam parked, and they stepped out to stretch their legs.

Josie bounded ahead on her leash, tail wagging like a banner.

"Worth it," Haylee said, admiring the view.

"Alright," Sam said eventually, "ready for the next stretch?"

Haylee nodded, brushing Bella's fur from her lap. "Let's keep going.

Under the Open Sky

That night, they pulled off onto a patch of public land, tucked between red rock formations and an endless sea of stars.

Haylee lit a small campfire while Sam prepped dinner from their stash.

"Careful with that skillet," she warned.

Too late—Sam dropped it into the fire.

"Oops."

Haylee doubled over laughing. "I thought you were the practical one."

"I am," he said, retrieving the scorched pan. "Just not when it comes to open flames."

Later, after dinner, they stretched out on a blanket beside the fire. The night air was cool, and the fire crackled quietly.

They lay in a gentle silence, stargazing. Sam's arm brushed against hers.

He shifted closer.

"Haylee?" he said softly.

She turned to him, eyes reflecting the stars.

He didn't speak right away. The moment stretched—comfortable, patient, electric.

Then he leaned in and kissed her.

It was tentative at first, a question.

When she kissed him back, it was an answer.

He pulled away just slightly, forehead resting against hers. "Was that okay?"

"Yeah," she whispered. "More than okay."

They sat together for a moment, hands laced between them.

Then Haylee murmured, "Maybe we should talk about what this means."

Sam smiled. "I think it means we're more than just traveling buddies."

Before anything more could be said, Josie barreled into them, tail wagging furiously, sending them both sprawling into a tangle of limbs and laughter.

"I guess she approves," Haylee laughed.

Sam grinned. "Definitely our best third wheel."

They eventually quieted, the fire burning low as the stars above shimmered endlessly.

Haylee stood and brushed off her jeans. "We should probably get some sleep."

"Yeah," Sam said, gathering their mugs and dousing the fire. As Sam began to make his bed on the pullout couch. Haylee interrupted.

"No... you can sleep in the bed, if you'd like. There's room. And it's warmer."

Sam looked at her carefully, reading her tone.

"You sure?"

Haylee nodded. "It's been a good day. I just... don't want it to end alone."

They climbed into the bed, Josie curling at their feet. Bella blinked at them sleepily from her perch near the window.

Under the soft lamplight, Haylee and Sam settled down. They didn't speak much. He wrapped an arm around her, and she tucked herself against his chest.

They lay that way for a long while—hearing only the faint wind outside, the creak of Bertha's frame cooling with the night, and the steady rhythm of each other's breath.

No expectations.

Just warmth.

Just peace.

Just the beginning of something real.

Roadside Omens

The next morning, they stopped at a quirky roadside stand that looked like it had been plucked straight from a storybook. An older woman sat at a table covered in handmade trinkets, jars of preserves, and a deck of tarot cards.

Haylee browsed absentmindedly until her eyes landed on a keychain—a small brass key, almost identical to one Aggie used to wear.

She picked it up.

"Something familiar?" the woman asked, her eyes sharp behind thick lenses.

"Just... looks like something I used to know."

The woman slid a tarot card from the deck—The Moon.

"Not everything hidden is meant to stay that way," she murmured.

Haylee blinked. "Excuse me?"

But the woman only smiled and handed her the keychain.

"No charge. Sometimes, the road wants you to have something."

Back in Bertha, Haylee ran her fingers over the key.

Sam gave her a look. "That mean something to you?"

"I'm not sure yet," she replied. "But maybe it will."

Chapter Ten:
Between the Lines

They packed up slowly, taking in the hush of early morning mist over the campground. A cool breeze threaded through the pine trees, and Haylee's playlist bounced through genres—folk to funk, classic rock to lo-fi jazz.

Sam raised an eyebrow. "Your taste in music is either chaotic or genius."

Haylee smirked, tossing a hoodie into Bertha's back bench. "That's the spirit of the road—unexpected, but somehow it all works."

As Bertha rumbled onto the open road, Haylee took the wheel again. Sam leaned back, one foot on the dash, sipping coffee from a dented metal thermos.

As Bertha rolled forward and the trees thinned beside the highway, Haylee kept her eyes on the winding road ahead.

This isn't just about finding direction anymore, she thought. It's about loving freely. Letting myself feel all of it—without fear.

Sam reached across the console, letting his hand rest briefly over hers. The silence said more than he could have.

They arrived at a quiet campground near a small river, nestled at the edge of a forested ridge. The air carried the scent of pine needles and damp moss, and the water's steady rush smoothed the edges of Haylee's thoughts.

She stood outside Bertha, cradling a mug of tea, watching the river's ripples. Sam stepped out, coffee in hand, his usual sleepy shuffle softening into stillness beside her.

"Good morning," he said, voice warm and just a little rough.

"Morning," Haylee replied, not taking her eyes off the river. "It's beautiful here."

Sam nodded and sat at the picnic table. "You doing okay?"

Haylee joined him, her shoulders relaxing. "Yeah. Really good."

There was peace between them—earned, not forced. For once, she wasn't bracing for what might happen next. But still, something nagged in the background: the mystery texts, the silence from Riles, the sense of eyes unseen.

Sam seemed to read her thoughts. "Want to talk about it?"

Haylee hesitated. Then nodded. "I'm scared. Scared of losing this. Of losing myself. Of not knowing what's around the corner."

Sam didn't flinch. He set his coffee down and placed his hand gently over hers.

"I get that. But I'm here for you."

Haylee looked down at their hands. "I don't want to shut myself off from something real just because I'm afraid of losing what I've built."

"You don't have to choose," Sam said. "You can be you. Strong, independent, stubborn—"

"Hey!"

He grinned. "—and still let someone care about you."

She laughed softly. The weight she'd been carrying felt lighter. Not gone—but shared.

They stayed at the river for two days. No pressure. Just space. Cooking, long walks with Josie, and Bella sunbathing on Bertha's dashboard.

When they left, they followed a coastal route until a salty breeze rolled in through the cracked windows. They'd reached a quiet oceanside town.

With Bertha parked close to the beach, waves thundering in a steady rhythm. Haylee and Sam stepped out, breathing in the salt and light.

Josie dashed forward, then halted as the water rolled in. Her paws danced backward, tail wagging with uncertainty.

Sam laughed. "You got this, girl!"

Haylee kicked off her sandals and ran to the shoreline, splashing water in Sam's direction.

He retaliated, and they played like kids until they collapsed on the wet sand, breathless with laughter.

Back near the RV, Bella tiptoed onto the sand, sniffed the salty breeze, then promptly darted back to the sink with a huff.

"I think she prefers mountain air," Haylee said.

"She's the real queen of the road," Sam replied.

Haylee looked out over the ocean. "Do you think we'll ever stop moving?"

Sam's answer was simple. "Not until we're ready."

53

That night, as the stars emerged one by one, Haylee and Sam lay side by side in Bertha's bed. No rush. Just quiet breathing, arms wrapped loosely around each other, the rhythm of the waves a lullaby. It was the soft, silent kind of closeness that didn't need words.

It was a perfect ending to a perfect day.

Chapter Eleven:
The Quirks of the Road

It had been a few days since they left the coastal town, and they'd meandered through winding roads, stopping in quirky little towns and small roadside diners. Today, they found themselves in a tiny desert town known for its "World's Largest Collection of Homemade Windchimes."

Haylee, ever the curious soul, insisted they stop. Sam wasn't opposed, but tourist traps weren't exactly his thing. Still, he didn't say so—he could see the excitement in her eyes.

The town was exactly what they expected: dusty, colorful, and full of character. Wind chimes hung everywhere—on shop porches, tree branches, and even the rusted walls of a run-down café. There was a quiet, nostalgic charm to it, like stepping back in time.

They wandered through town, Haylee snapping photos of the strangest and most whimsical chimes, laughing at the quirky signs like "Do not disturb the wind, it is busy," and "Wind Chimes: Not just for Trees."

Then came the sign that sealed the deal:

"Come Try the World's Largest Wind Chime — Play With It!"

"Do you think it's real?" Haylee asked, her eyes wide with anticipation.

Sam shrugged. "Only one way to find out."

They followed a cactus-lined path to a clearing, where a massive wooden frame held metal tubes taller than either of them. It looked like something straight out of a whimsical fever dream.

Haylee darted forward. "This is insane! I have to try it."

Before Sam could reply, she grabbed the largest tube and gave it a hearty swing. The deep, resonant chime echoed through the open lot, vibrating in their chests.

"Whoa," Sam said, grinning. "That's some serious chime power."

Haylee tried another, accidentally setting off a chaotic medley of clangs. The symphony was so loud and erratic, she froze.

"Uh-oh."

But instead of complaints, a small crowd gathered—laughing, clapping, enjoying the noise.

An older man with a grizzled beard approached, clapping along. "You've done it! Broken the sound barrier with chimes!"

"I didn't mean to—" Haylee started.

The man winked. "No worries. You brought them to life. Help me tune 'em and I'll let you play the finale."

What followed was a hilarious hour of tuning, adjusting, and improvising. Sam captured it all on video—Haylee helping the man, leading tourists in an impromptu "chime chorus," and soaking in every odd moment.

Back at the RV, Haylee bounced into Bertha with renewed energy. "This has to go on YouTube."

Sam chuckled. "Good thing I filmed everything."

She stopped, eyeing him. "Wait, really?"

He showed her the footage.

Haylee squealed and launched into his arms, peppering his face with kisses. "You're the best!"

Sam blushed, but it didn't last—he kissed her back, playfully, sweetly.

For a brief, shining moment, there was nothing but laughter and windchimes echoing in their memory.

As they continued down the road, the adventure didn't let up.

They passed through sleepy mountain towns with cafes so hidden, you'd miss them if you blinked. At one, the coffee was so strong Sam joked it could "raise the dead and then give them a second wind."

Outside a rustic café, he spotted a bright yellow flyer taped to a cracked bulletin board.

"The Greatest Cactus Parade — This Weekend Only!"

The parade, held in a tiny valley town, featured giant cacti dressed up like parade floats—hats, scarves, sunglasses, even feather boas. Somehow, Haylee and Sam got roped into helping decorate one with a group of strangers. By the end, their cactus was wearing aviator goggles, a bandana, and a "Keep On Rollin'" bumper sticker.

"I don't know if I'm proud or slightly concerned," Sam said, stepping back to admire their creation.

"I'm both," Haylee replied, snapping a picture.

It was absurd. It was delightful. Their inner children were absolutely thriving.

But the real highlights weren't just the events—they were the people.

At a quiet lakeside campground, they met a woman named Ellie who lived in a converted ambulance. Her traveling companion? A parrot named Oscar, who instantly mimicked Haylee's laugh with eerie accuracy.

Haylee doubled over. "Oh my god, does he do this to everyone?"

Ellie grinned. "Only the ones he likes."

Sam eyed the bird warily. "What's Oscar's story?"

Ellie leaned against the open ambulance door. "Retired circus performer. Now he travels with me and dispenses completely unhinged life advice."

"Like what?" Haylee asked, still giggling.

"Yesterday he told me to buy more duct tape and start a fire," Ellie said with a shrug and a wink. "So, you know. Proceed with caution."

Sam let out a loud, unapologetic laugh. "Well there it is—wisdom from a retired circus parrot."

Oscar flapped his wings and screeched, "DO IT!"

They all burst out laughing, the sound echoing across the lake.

Chapter Twelve:
Soak, Sunsets and Serendipity

One of the most memorable stops came in a tiny desert town known for its hot springs.

Haylee and Sam arrived just as the sky turned gold, the last of the sunlight draping the mountains in amber shadows. After settling into a cozy campsite tucked beneath cottonwoods, they grabbed towels and walked to the springs, steam already curling like wisps of magic into the evening air.

The water was warm, soothing every mile of the road from their limbs. As they soaked beneath the painted sky—blush oranges melting into lavender clouds—Haylee leaned her head back, eyes half-closed, her fingers brushing gently against Sam's under the surface.

Neither of them spoke for a while. They didn't need to. The warmth of the water, the quiet of dusk, the nearness of each other—it said everything.

The perfect ending to a beautiful day.

The next morning, while packing up Bertha, a couple approached them from across the gravel lot—smiling, breathless, and clearly excited.

"Hey!" the man called. "We were just talking about you two!"

Haylee blinked, caught off guard. "Us?"

"You're the wind chime duo, right?" the woman added, grinning. "We saw the YouTube video. That chaos with the giant chimes? Totally made our week."

Haylee's eyes widened. "You saw my channel?"

"Small world," the woman said, laughing. "And *you're* Sam the dog bather!"

Sam rubbed the back of his neck with a sheepish grin. "Yep. Pets sprayed by skunks—that's kind of my specialty now."

They all laughed.

Introductions were exchanged, and soon they were swapping stories, contacts, and Instagram handles. The couple—Jess and Theo—were also nomads, traveling in a retro pop-up camper with a solar panel strapped to the roof and a travel-sized espresso machine proudly bungee-corded to the counter.

"We figured if we're going to live on the road," Jess said, "we're doing it caffeinated."

As they talked, Haylee marveled at the strange and beautiful way the road wove lives together. You could drive hundreds of miles and not see a soul, and then —suddenly—you'd meet someone who felt like an old friend. A familiar echo in the wilderness.

"You never know who you'll meet or where," Haylee said later, once Jess and Theo had headed out. "But when it happens, it always feels like the road meant it that way."

Sam nodded, tossing a duffel into Bertha. "The road's got good timing."

Signs in Passing

Later that afternoon, the road stretched long and quiet, rolling over low hills and through sun-bleached fields. Sam had taken the wheel, Bertha humming contentedly beneath him while Haylee lounged in the passenger seat, scribbling notes in her journal.

Josie was sprawled across the floor, snoring softly. Bella, as usual, had claimed the dashboard, her tail flicking like a metronome to the music drifting from the speakers.

Haylee glanced up from her notebook. "You know, I've seen more oddly shaped clouds today than in the last year combined."

Sam grinned. "That one looks like a walrus doing yoga."

Haylee laughed. "You're ridiculous."

"Just trying to keep us entertained. This stretch of road is doing its best to bore me into a nap."

Then, just as the laughter died down, something caught Haylee's eye through the passenger-side window. A faded wooden sign, nearly swallowed by tall grass and brush, flashed by.

She turned back quickly. "Wait—did that sign say Key Keepers Welcome?"

Sam squinted in the rearview mirror. "Didn't see it. Want me to turn around?"

Haylee hesitated. Her instincts buzzed, but she didn't feel ready to veer off course.

"No… not yet. It was probably nothing. Just… odd."

She jotted the words in the margin of her journal without explanation.

A few miles later, they pulled into a rest stop to stretch their legs. As they walked Josie around the gravel path behind a picnic area, Haylee noticed something etched into the back of a metal road sign. Just a faint outline—but it struck her.

A symbol she recognized from her dream back at the café. A swirling line through a circle, just like the one in Aggie's journal.

She touched it lightly with her fingers, heart ticking a little faster.

"You okay?" Sam asked from a few feet away, noticing her pause.

"Yeah," Haylee said, too quickly. Then, more slowly: "I think this road is going to show us more than we expect."

Sam didn't press, but his expression softened. He reached for her hand as they walked back toward Bertha.

Chapter Thirteen:
Christmas and Crossroads

With Christmas only a few days away, Haylee had told her dad she'd be at a national park for the holiday. She hadn't expected him to actually show up.

One afternoon, after a long hike through the nearby woods—with Sam beside her and Josie bounding ahead—they returned to find David waiting by the RV.

Haylee stopped in her tracks. "Dad?"

David stood with his arms crossed, casual but clearly observant. "Hi. I'm David," he said, stepping forward and offering a hand. "Haylee's father."

Sam looked slightly caught off guard but recovered quickly. He extended his hand. "I'm Sam. Nice to meet you, sir."

David gave Sam a once-over, subtle but thorough. Haylee noticed. The tension wasn't aggressive—more like two men trying to quietly measure one another. Josie trotted up with a stick clamped between her teeth, her tongue lolling out, tail wagging furiously. She dropped the stick at David's feet, looking from him to Sam.

David chuckled, the ice breaking just a little. "I come bearing gifts," he said, motioning to a nearby bag, "but I wasn't aware you had company."

Haylee stepped in. "Thank you, Dad. And yeah, Sam's been traveling with me."

Sam scratched the back of his neck. "Don't worry about me, sir. I don't really celebrate Christmas anyway."

Haylee and David both turned to look at him, eyebrows raised.

Sam shrugged. "Not for any particular reason—just never got into the tradition."

The moment was awkward but not uncomfortable. No one pressed further. Sam unlocked Bertha and Josie hopped inside with practiced ease.

"I'll get started on dinner," Sam offered, disappearing into the RV.

Haylee made coffee over the small propane stove while David laid out the modest gifts he'd brought—nothing extravagant, but thoughtful. As the meal cooked over the open fire pit, they all sat together and simply talked. Not everything was easy, and not everything was said, but it felt real. And to Haylee, that was what mattered.

As Sam tended the food—carefully turning it so it wouldn't burn, again—David leaned in close to Haylee and spoke low, so only she could hear.

"We need to talk. Alone."

Haylee gave a small smile and shook her head. "Dad, it's okay. Sam knows everything."

David raised an eyebrow.

"And we have something to tell you too," she added, glancing toward Sam with a mixture of warmth and certainty.

The conversation was far from over—but this time, Haylee wasn't hiding, and she wasn't standing alone.

Beneath the Surface

Later that evening, the three of them gathered by the fire, coffee mugs in hand. The conversation turned more serious.

Sam set down his cup. "There's something you should know. The night before we went to the police station, I saw someone outside the RV. A dark figure—just standing there. When I went out to check, the footprints led up to Bertha… but didn't go anywhere. It was like they vanished."

David frowned, eyes narrowing. "Vanished? No tracks leading away?"

Sam nodded. "Exactly. And then there was that knock at my apartment—same day. I checked, no one was there. Same feeling. Something was off."

Haylee picked up from there. "And the tracker we found under Bertha—it just fell off one day. Detective Riles says it's military grade. Not something a casual stalker would use."

David exhaled slowly, eyes on the fire. "I'm not surprised."

Haylee tilted her head. "Why not?"

"Old Navy buddy of mine looked into it. After I saw you last, I asked him to dig around. That tech isn't exactly new—but it's rare, expensive, and hard to get without connections. Someone had resources. And that someone... might just be Elliot."

Sam leaned forward. "So, what's the deal with Elliot? Who is he really?"

David hesitated, gaze hardening. "He's connected to Aggie—more than I understood back then. She was hiding things, even from me. And Elliot? The few people who knew him said he was obsessed with finding something. Something beyond this world."

Haylee exchanged a look with Sam. "Like the dreams I've been having... the symbols?"

Sam nodded. "It's all tied together. I think it's time we talk to Riles again—see what he's really holding back."

David looked at them both, curious. "What symbols?"

Haylee reached into a small drawer inside Bertha and returned with the medallion. She handed it to her father.

"I've been having these dreams about a symbol. Then we found this in a hidden compartment inside the RV," she said.

David turned the medallion over in his hands, the firelight catching on its strange etchings. "I've never seen anything like this. It just... showed up?"

Sam nodded. "Bella found the hiding spot. We never noticed it before."

The fire crackled between them, but a different kind of spark had ignited. They weren't just chasing clues now—they were stepping into a deeper mystery. And Haylee wasn't walking into it alone.

Later that evening

After her dad had gone to bed and the fire had burned down to glowing embers, Haylee and Sam sat in comfortable silence beneath a sky full of stars. The air was still, peaceful, wrapped in the kind of quiet that only comes after a long, meaningful day.

Haylee drew in a slow breath, letting it out with a sense of ease she hadn't felt in a long while. For the first time in what felt like forever, she could breathe— really breathe. The weight of the past, the unknowns, the tangled threads of truth and fear—they weren't gone, but they weren't suffocating her either.

She glanced over at Sam. His silhouette was soft in the starlight, calm and familiar. He didn't say anything—he didn't have to. His presence was enough.

She wasn't alone anymore.

The road ahead, with all its twists, shadows, and unexpected turns, didn't seem so daunting. Not with Sam beside her. Not with Josie curled at their feet, the fire crackling low, and the promise of something real growing between them.

The future was uncertain.

But it was hers to share.

And with that simple truth, Haylee felt ready—finally ready—to take the next step.

Chapter Fourteen:
Between Breakfast and Truth

The next morning, Haylee woke to find Sam and her dad outside, deep in conversation. She lingered in the doorway of Bertha, quietly watching them. Two men—different in so many ways—but both, in their own quiet way, made her feel safe. She found herself wishing she could freeze the moment. Just for a little while.

Josie, ever the lookout, spotted her and gave a soft chuff before stretching and sitting up. Sam and David turned at once.

"Morning," they called out in unison.

It caught them all off guard. The awkward pause that followed was broken by Haylee's easy laughter.

"Morning to you too," she grinned, stepping outside.

They gathered around the fire pit for breakfast—omelets filled with peppers, onions, and chopped-up leftovers from the night before. Something simple, but good. Something comforting before what came next.

Because once the plates were scraped clean and the coffee cups were full again, they all knew what was waiting on the other end of a phone call.

Detective Riles.

The Line Between

David pulled out his phone and gave Haylee a look. "It's time," he said.

Haylee hesitated, then nodded. She handed over the detective's number, and David stepped away to make the call, pacing slowly along the edge of the campground.

Sam and Haylee watched from a distance, reading his body language more than his words. His brows furrowed. He stopped pacing once. Then again.

When David returned, he didn't sit down right away. Instead, he crossed his arms, gaze unreadable. "Riles wants to meet. Somewhere neutral. Tomorrow morning, back near town."

"What did he say?" Haylee asked.

"Not much over the phone. But I pushed. Told him I knew more about Elliot than I let on. That got his attention."

Sam shifted. "You think he knows Elliot?"

David shook his head. "He didn't say. But I caught something in his voice— hesitation. Not fear, exactly. Like he's walking a line."

"A line between what?" Haylee asked.

David sat slowly. "Between helping us and protecting himself. My guess? Riles has already stirred something up. He said his access to internal files was restricted shortly after our last visit. He's been trying to dig deeper into Aggie's case, and someone's making that hard."

"Someone above him?" Sam asked.

"Maybe not directly. He's not even sure. Could be coming from someone higher up the chain—or someone with ties outside the department. He said the phrase 'I was told to stop asking.'"

Haylee's stomach dropped. "So, whoever is involved… they have reach."

David nodded. "And Riles? I think he knows he's in over his head. But he's not stopping."

Sam rubbed his jaw. "Then we shouldn't either."

David glanced at the medallion again, still resting on the picnic table between them. "Whatever this is—it's bigger than Aggie, bigger than Elliot. Riles may not know who he's protecting, but he's close to figuring it out."

Haylee looked at them both. "Then tomorrow, we go meet him. All of us."

Shadows at the Edge

They arrived in the nearby town just before noon, settling into a quiet corner booth of a small diner with fogged windows and the scent of fresh coffee lingering in the air. The place felt neutral—unremarkable in all the right ways. No one paid much attention to the trio who walked in, and that's exactly what they were hoping for.

Riles arrived not long after. He looked tired—more so than the last time they'd seen him. His coat was wrinkled, his hair a little unkempt, and his eyes constantly scanned the windows.

"Thanks for coming," he said, sliding into the booth across from them.

David gave a small nod. "You said you had something. Let's not dance around it."

Riles hesitated, glancing toward the door before lowering his voice. "I shouldn't even be here. Things have gotten… complicated."

Haylee leaned in. "What does that mean?"

"I've been locked out of several databases since our last conversation. My inquiries about Aggie's past and her connections to Elliot were flagged. I don't know by who—just that I was told to stop asking."

David's voice was low but firm. "You stirred the wrong pot."

Riles nodded. "I thought I was dealing with something small. A tracker, a missing person. But this goes deeper. The tech under Bertha? That's not civilian-grade. It's military-adjacent. And the request to access it didn't come from inside my department. It came from a blacked-out node. Third-party, likely private security—but with government clearance."

Sam exhaled sharply. "So, someone powerful wanted to keep tabs on Aggie."

"And now you," Riles said, looking at Haylee. "I have a theory. I can't prove it, but everything I've found points to someone with influence... and obsession."

"Elliot," David said quietly.

Riles looked at him. "That name keeps circling back, even when I try to follow unrelated leads. People who knew Aggie won't talk—or they disappear. And this tracker? I traced one similar model back to a case that was sealed two decades ago. Code-named 'VEIL.'"

Haylee felt her skin prickle. "Veil?"

Riles nodded slowly. "I don't know what it means. But it was buried deep. Someone didn't want it found."

Before anyone could speak again, the bell over the diner door jingled. A man in a black ball cap stepped inside, glanced once around the room, then took a seat at the counter without ordering anything.

Riles noticed. His expression stiffened. "I was followed."

David's tone hardened. "You're sure?"

"I parked two blocks over. Took the long way. Still, someone tracked me here."

Haylee's heart began to race. "So now what?"

Riles didn't answer right away. His eyes met hers, and for the first time, he looked genuinely unnerved. "Now? We all walk out separately. Get in your RV. Drive. But stay off the radar. Whoever Elliot is, whatever he's after—he's close. Closer than you think."

Sam's hand instinctively brushed against Haylee's under the table, a silent reassurance.

David spoke with quiet authority. "We regroup. Somewhere safe. And we plan."

Riles gave a single nod.

"And don't lose that medallion. Whatever it is—he wants it. Badly."

As Haylee, Sam, and David left through the back, Riles lingered.

He spotted the man near the counter. Ball cap. Silent. Waiting.

Riles didn't hesitate. He followed the man out into the alley behind the diner. "What's your problem?" Riles demanded.

The man turned with a sneer. "Should've minded your own business."

Riles struck first. The fight was fast and brutal—gritty, no finesse. Riles wasn't a brawler, but he knew how to hold his own. The other guy didn't expect that. When it was over, the man was down and groaning, and Riles was limping. He wiped blood from his lip, breathing hard. "You tell whoever sent you— they're not scaring me off."

Back at the RV, Haylee, Sam, and David drove off in tense silence. None of them had seen what happened. But they could feel it—something had shifted. And whatever they were chasing… it was now chasing them back.

Chapter Fifteen:
The Quiet Between

They drove in silence, the weight of the diner meeting settling over them like fog. No one spoke—not because there was nothing to say, but because none of them knew where to begin.

After a couple of hours on the road, they found a small, out-of-the-way campground that barely registered on the GPS. Nestled among tall pines and bordered by a slow-moving river, the place looked abandoned, like nature had half taken it back—but a small wooden sign near the entrance simply read: **"OPEN. HONOR SYSTEM."**

It was perfect.

They parked Bertha under a canopy of pines and stretched their legs. The quiet here wasn't just peaceful—it felt protective.

There was something calming about the overgrown edges, the worn fire rings, the faint sound of water lapping against smooth stones. It was the kind of place that asked no questions.

As Josie sniffed around and Bella curled up inside, Haylee started the kettle and Sam got a fire going. David wandered a little but stayed within earshot.

Once they settled, Sam got a small fire going while Haylee and David unpacked a few things from the RV. The air was cooler here, the river offering a subtle, soothing rush that seemed to mask the hum of unease they all carried.

David pulled out his phone to text Riles—but a reply came quickly and unexpectedly.

Do not text this number again. I'm getting a burner. I think my phone was compromised. Will reach out when I can.

David held the screen out for them to see. "He's being cautious—smart. If they followed him once, they could be tracing his phone."

Sam exhaled sharply. "That means we wait."

Haylee nodded, though the knot in her stomach tightened. "Do you think we should talk about what he told us? At the diner?"

David looked between them. "Yeah. We should."

They gathered closer to the fire, the quiet sounds of nature amplifying every word.

A few hours went by, David checked his phone again, then frowned. "Still nothing from Riles."

Haylee sipped her tea, eyes on the fire. "He said he'd get a burner, right?"

David nodded slowly. "Yeah. If someone had eyes on him, his phone was probably compromised."

"So now what?" Sam asked.

David didn't answer right away. He looked up, meeting both their eyes. "We talk about what we know. Riles gave us more than he realized."

Haylee wrapped her arms around her knees. "Like how Elliot is still out there. And after something."

David leaned forward. "Not just something. The medallion."

Sam reached into Bertha and retrieved it, placing it on the wooden picnic table beside them. Its surface shimmered faintly in the firelight.

"I didn't tell you everything earlier," David said, his voice lower now. "When I was still in the Navy, I heard rumors—fringe stuff. Not officially acknowledged. Symbols. Portals. Tech that didn't act like tech. And there was one name that came up more than once: Elliot."

Haylee's heart jumped. "You think he's not... just a man?"

"I think Aggie knew something. Something dangerous enough to hide this from everyone—even me."

Sam's voice was steady. "Riles said the tracker was military-grade. But what if Elliot's using people in places we can't see? What if this isn't just about tracking Aggie... or Haylee?"

David exhaled. "Then we're already on borrowed time."

They all sat in silence, listening to the fire crackle.

Then Haylee spoke, her voice calm but resolute. "This medallion. He wants it because it's the key to something."

"To becoming something," David clarified. "Not just crossing over—but staying. Forever."

"Immortal?" Sam asked, brow furrowed.

David nodded once. "That's what my buddy thinks. Elliot isn't just powerful— he's dangerous. He was banished from this realm once, by Aggie. If he gets his hands on that medallion... it might not be possible to stop him again."

Haylee touched the medallion's edge. "Then we keep it hidden. And we stay ahead."

Sam looked up at her. "We're not just running anymore. We're guarding something."

"No," Haylee said, eyes meeting his. "We're protecting more than just ourselves now."

David leaned back, the weight of their new reality settling around them like the darkness creeping through the trees.

For now, they were safe.

But Elliot was out there.

And he was watching.

In the silence, the trees whispered secrets—and somewhere far off, Elliot was already listening.

Chapter Sixteen:
Breathing Space

The next morning arrived like any other—soft light breaking through the tall trees, dew on the grass, the faint sound of the river nearby. The tension from the day before hadn't disappeared, but something had shifted. Haylee felt it in her chest, subtle but unmistakable. Even Josie and Bella seemed calmer, as if the stillness of the forest had wrapped itself around them all.

She padded to the RV's door, stretching. Through the window, she spotted Sam already outside, coffee in hand, tending to the little camp stove.

He caught sight of her and grinned. "Good morning, sunshine."

Haylee smiled back, pulling on her hoodie. The crisp morning air greeted her like an old friend. David was still asleep inside, phone clutched loosely in one hand, the weight of yesterday pressing on him even in rest.

She joined Sam by the fire ring, accepting a mug of coffee that was, thankfully, strong and hot. They sat in silence for a few beats, steam curling from their cups, the forest slowly coming alive around them.

Sam finally spoke. "So… what's the plan? We can't exactly sit around waiting for Riles to call."

Haylee took another sip and exhaled slowly. "Agreed. I don't want to spend the whole day holding our breath."

"I saw a trailhead nearby," Sam said, nodding toward the trees. "Supposedly ends at a waterfall. You in?"

Haylee looked down at Josie, who was enthusiastically chewing a leaf like it was the best breakfast ever. "I think that's a yes from her."

They shared a laugh—small, real, necessary.

Haylee leaned into the back of her camp chair and looked up at the clear sky.

The Calm we keep

Back inside the RV, David stirred awake and stretched. The smell of fresh coffee lingered, but no one was around.

On the small table, he found a neatly written note:

"Gone for a short hike. Be back for lunch. – H&S"

David ran a hand through his hair and let out a soft sigh. He picked up his phone and set it beside him, keeping it close in case Riles called. Then he moved to the front of the RV and settled into the passenger seat. Bella was already there, sprawled out in her favorite sunny patch on the dash, eyes closed in complete feline contentment.

He chuckled softly. "You've got it all figured out, don't you, cat?"

The solitude gave him time to reflect—on the past few days, the strange symbols, the tracker, and the tension building around Elliot's name. Something bigger was at play, and it was starting to feel like the threads were pulling tighter around them all.

Still, for now, the RV was quiet, warm, and safe. And in that moment of stillness, David let himself breathe.

Haylee, Sam, and Josie followed the narrow trail through the woods, the morning sun casting golden rays through the tall trees. The sounds of birds and the crunch of gravel underfoot were the only company they needed. After the tension of the past few days, the simplicity of this hike felt like a balm.

The trail led them to a secluded waterfall—a soft cascade spilling over smooth rock into a crystal-clear pool below. The air here was damp and fresh, charged with the scent of moss and pine.

Haylee kicked off her boots, laughing as Josie barreled straight into the water. "She's braver than both of us," Sam said, setting down his pack.

Haylee stepped into the shallows, the water cold at first, then invigorating. Sam joined her, and soon they were splashing each other, laughter echoing off the rocks.

After a while, the energy between them shifted—still light, but more intimate. Haylee paused, water glistening on her skin, her gaze locked on Sam's. The world quieted around them.

He moved closer, brushing wet strands of hair from her face.

Their kiss was slow and deep, a meeting of something long building between them. They moved together gently in the water, the current swirling around their legs. It wasn't rushed or careless—it was soft, sacred. A moment entirely their own.

Later, wrapped in towels and watching Josie chase shadows on the bank, Haylee leaned into Sam's shoulder.

"That felt… like more than I expected," she said.

Sam kissed the top of her head. "Me too."

They sat in silence for a while, the waterfall still humming behind them, a quiet pulse of something wild and steady.

The world hadn't changed—but they had.

81

And when they finally gathered their things to head back, there was a deeper stillness between them. One not born from fear or uncertainty—but from something true, something shared.

Something that could last.

Chapter Seventeen:
When the Light Shifts

David had received a text from Riles earlier that morning, but he didn't say anything—not right away. Not when he looked up and saw Haylee and Sam returning from their hike, hand in hand.

There was something different about them. The way they moved together, the way they smiled without speaking. It wasn't just affection—it was certainty, a quiet bond forged in something deeper than just miles on the road.

David watched for a moment longer, his jaw tight. He didn't want to be the one to shatter the calm, but reality rarely waited for perfect timing.

"Morning," Haylee called cheerfully, a lightness in her step.

"Morning," David echoed, standing and brushing the dust off his jeans. "We need to talk."

Haylee's smile faded, replaced by concern. Sam's brows drew together.

David got straight to the point. "Riles texted. He's on his way here. Should be joining us for dinner tonight."

Sam's eyes flicked to Haylee's. "That's soon."

"Yeah. He didn't want to say much in the text. Said it's better we talk in person." David's voice lowered. "He sounded... different. Cautious."

Josie flopped by the firepit with a soft huff, as if the weight of the moment settled on her too.

Haylee stared into the flames that hadn't yet been lit. "Do you think something's wrong?"

David nodded, almost imperceptibly. "I think something's already in motion."

Quiet Before the Storm

The day moved slowly, as if the air itself were holding its breath. Sam gathered kindling while Haylee rinsed dishes at the water spigot nearby, each of them going through the motions but clearly somewhere else in their thoughts. Even Josie seemed more subdued, resting beneath the picnic table, her ears twitching at the slightest sound.

David sat in a folding chair near the fire pit, legs stretched out, eyes scanning the tree line. He hadn't said much since dropping the news about Riles. He kept his phone close, checking it often, though no new messages came.

Haylee returned with the last of the clean mugs, setting them down with more force than necessary. "It's too quiet," she muttered.

Sam looked up from the fire he was coaxing to life. "You mean peaceful?"

"No. I mean the kind of quiet that feels like something's coming. Like the air's too still."

David finally spoke. "That's because something is coming."

Haylee crossed her arms. "You think Riles is bringing trouble?"

"I think," David said slowly, "that trouble's already found him. And if he's right… we're next."

They all went silent again, the weight of that statement hanging heavily. The fire popped, sending a few sparks upward, but no one moved to speak.

Bella padded out of Bertha and perched on the RV steps, her golden eyes locked on the trees. She rarely came out like this unless something had her attention.

"Maybe we should have left after the hike," Sam said, glancing at Haylee.

"Maybe we should have left after the hike," Sam said, glancing at Haylee.

"No," she said, shaking her head. "We stay. We face this."

David gave a small nod of approval. "Just be ready for anything."

The wind stirred the trees. Somewhere in the distance, a crow called out once and then fell silent.

Even the forest seemed to know something was about to change.

Into the Firelight

That evening, as the sun dipped behind the trees, casting long golden shadows across the forest floor, the three of them moved around camp with an unspoken rhythm. Sam tended to the fire, coaxing it to life with careful hands, while Haylee prepped vegetables and handed David a cutting board.

Dinner was a quiet choreography—nothing fancy, but something warm and grounding. They sat in a loose circle around the fire pit, waiting.

It wasn't long before the crunch of gravel and the low hum of a engine signaled Riles' arrival. The headlights flickered through the trees before a dusty Jeep pulled into view. Riles stepped out, his posture tight, his eyes scanning the clearing with practiced vigilance.

He looked exhausted—unshaven, shirt slightly wrinkled, a man who hadn't slept in more than a day.

"Evening," he said, voice low and hoarse.

Haylee stood, her concern plain. "You okay?"

Riles gave a short nod. "Had to be careful getting here. Took a few backroads. Think I lost them."

Sam exchanged a glance with David. "Them?"

Riles didn't answer right away. He walked closer to the fire, the warmth seeming to hit him all at once. He sank into a camp chair with a sigh.

"I don't have long," he said. "But I have answers."

Truths in the Smoke

Riles leaned forward, rubbing his hands together like he needed the fire to chase something colder than the night air.

"I started digging deeper after our last conversation," he said, his voice low. "Trying to figure out who had access to that tracking tech. It's not standard issue—not for law enforcement, not for civilian use. My contact in DC confirmed it was military-grade, maybe even black ops level. Only thing that makes sense is that someone high up authorized it… or someone off the books did."

David tensed. "And Elliot?"

Riles nodded slowly. "Every time I ran his name, doors closed. My access was revoked on certain files. Got a warning from my captain to 'let it go.' But I didn't. I kept pushing."

Sam's jaw tightened. "And that's why someone followed you."

Riles gave a dry chuckle. "Yeah. I got too close. Asked the wrong questions. Stepped on the wrong toes. I wasn't even digging into criminal charges—just trying to map connections between Aggie, Elliot, and a few people in intelligence."

Haylee frowned. "So what *did* you find?"

Riles hesitated. Then: "Elliot's not just some off-the-grid eccentric. He was involved in classified research decades ago—psychological ops, experimental testing, fringe science. He disappeared from official records fifteen years ago, right around the time Aggie broke contact with almost everyone."

David shifted. "My buddy said Aggie was involved in something too. Something she never talked about."

Riles nodded again. "She was. I think she turned on Elliot. Tried to stop whatever he was chasing."

Haylee's eyes flicked toward the RV. "The medallion."

"That's the theory," Riles said. "What you found? That's not just a keepsake. It's a key. Elliot's trying to come back in a real, physical way. And if he gets that medallion, he won't just be dangerous—he'll be unstoppable."

Silence settled over the camp like a weighted blanket. The fire popped and cracked, but no one moved.

Finally, Haylee broke the stillness. "So what do we do now?"

Riles met her gaze. "You stay mobile. Stay quiet. And you don't let that medallion out of your sight."

He looked at all of them.

"And whatever happens—don't trust anyone unless you know exactly where they stand."

Just as Riles stood to leave, brushing soot from his jacket, he turned toward his Jeep—then paused.

A couple was approaching the site from the far end of the trail. They looked to be in their mid-thirties, sun-kissed and comfortably worn in the way only seasoned travelers seemed to be. The woman had a flannel shirt tied around her waist, and the man carried a small mesh bag filled with marshmallows and graham crackers.

Riles instinctively shifted his stance, scanning them with a weariness that hadn't left him since he arrived.

Sam caught the change and held up a hand with a grin. "Stand down, Columbo."

The woman waved as they neared. "Hey, mind if we join you?" Her voice was light, genuine. "Our firepit is overrun with ants, and we saw your fire."

"We brought stuff to make s'mores," the man added, holding up the bag like a peace offering.

Haylee glanced at David and Sam, then smiled. "Of course. Always nice to meet fellow travelers."

Riles gave a tight nod, his eyes still scanning the woods behind them. "Good night," he said quietly to the group. "I'll be in touch. Don't contact me first."

Then he turned and disappeared into the dark, the Jeep's taillights vanishing between the trees—leaving behind the faint scent of firewood, mystery, and the echo of something just beginning to unfold.

Chapter Eighteen:
Kindred Roads

The new couple introduced themselves as Lily and Jack, and within moments, stories were flowing as easily as the coffee in their tin mugs. The two had been traveling together for years, hopping between national parks and stretches of BLM land. They rarely stayed at paid campgrounds, though this one—quiet, tucked under tall trees—had won them over for the night.

Their stories were met with genuine laughter and curiosity, the kind that lifted everyone's spirits. It was exactly what Haylee, Sam, and David needed after days of unease and revelations.

"You know," Lily said thoughtfully, poking at the fire with a long stick, "it's important to take time for yourself. Most people spend their lives rushing, trying to make money or keep up with other people's expectations. But that's not really living."

"Living," she continued, her gaze soft but steady, "is about being present. About letting a moment—like this one—just be enough."

Jack nodded, stretching his legs out by the fire. "Exactly. We used to be all about the hustle—corporate jobs, meetings, spreadsheets. But we weren't happy. So, we sold it all and left. Been on the road ever since. The freedom? It's addictive. And the road—man, it teaches you things."

Haylee listened, deeply moved. There was truth in what they were saying. The road had already given her so much: space to breathe, to question, to grow—and to connect. And she'd done it all on her own terms.

She glanced at Sam beside her, then across the fire at her father, who—despite his quiet nature—was watching Lily and Jack with a kind of reverence. Even David, for all his caution, seemed to be soaking in the energy around the fire.

"We've met a lot of people out here," Jack added, "but it's rare you stumble across the right ones at the right time."

Haylee smiled. "I believe that."

The fire crackled. Bella purred in her perch by Bertha's window. Josie dozed near the fire, twitching occasionally in a dream. The stars stretched endlessly overhead.

And in that small, glowing circle of travelers—new friends and old—the tension of the last few days loosened, just a little. Whatever was coming next, Haylee knew they'd face it with full hearts, open eyes, and company worth keeping.

In the Quiet Hours

As the fire dwindled to soft embers and the laughter faded into a comfortable silence, the evening began to settle like a warm blanket around the group. One by one, they said their goodnights. Lily and Jack disappeared into their converted van. David climbed onto the pull-out couch inside Bertha, Josie curling up beside him as if she'd been waiting for just that invitation. Bella, ever the creature of habit, nestled into the kitchen sink—her throne of comfort.

Haylee and Sam made their way to the back of the RV. The space was small, but it held a kind of intimacy that made it feel like a world of its own. They didn't speak much—there was no need. They undressed quietly, slid under the covers, and folded into each other with ease born from days on the road, shared looks, and stories whispered into night air.

In the quiet dark, their bodies found a familiar rhythm. Not the urgency of fear or longing, but something slower. Sweeter. A confirmation.

Their eyes met in the dim light spilling in from a nearby window, and no words were needed. There was love there, unspoken but undeniable. In the gentle brush of fingers against skin. In the way Haylee pressed her forehead to Sam's. In the steady, grounding beat of his heart beneath her palm.

Here, in this fragile calm between what had been and what might come, they found peace.

They would face what was next together.

Always.

Chapter Nineteen:
Where the Shadows Wait

Over breakfast, the trio sat around Bertha's folding table with paper plates in hand—scrambled eggs, toast, and fresh coffee. A lightness still lingered from the night before, but there was a flicker of restlessness beneath the surface.

"So," Sam said, stirring sugar into his mug, "what's the plan? We going to keep heading west or let the road surprise us?"

"I vote for surprise," Haylee said. "Feels like we've been following clues for so long. Maybe it's time we just… drive."

David nodded slowly. "A little distance isn't a bad thing."

They packed up camp and hit the road, Bertha humming as she curved along scenic highways. That afternoon, they passed through a town bustling with activity—colorful banners stretched across the street and glowing lanterns lined the sidewalks.

"Festival of Lights," Sam read from a sign. "Looks like we found our surprise."

The town was alive with music, food vendors, and laughter. String lights crisscrossed overhead, casting a magical glow over the crowd. They joined the revelers, moving between booths, dancing to street performers, and letting the joy of the moment carry them.

Josie trotted closely by Haylee's side, alert but content. David ducked into a booth to grab drinks for everyone.

Haylee was mid-laugh, swaying with Sam to the rhythm of a live band, when she felt a hand grip her arm—tight.

She turned.

Elliot.

His face was gaunt, eyes too sharp, too bright. "Come with me," he whispered, tugging her arm.

Before she could respond, Josie erupted in a bark that split through the music like lightning. Sam turned just in time to see Haylee being pulled away.

"HEY!" Sam lunged forward, shoving Elliot back.

The crowd turned. Chaos bloomed.

Elliot snarled—not like a man, but something else—and for a moment, Sam swore the shadows behind his eyes twisted. But Elliot was weaker here, tethered to this plane but not fully part of it.

Sam struck him hard. Elliot staggered, then vanished into the crowd like smoke. Haylee clutched Sam's jacket, shaking. David returned, eyes wide, taking it all in.

"We need to go," Sam said. "Now."

As they pushed their way through the crowd, the truth began to set in—not only did Elliot want the medallion… he wanted Haylee.

And he was willing to cross any line to get her.

After the Smoke Clears

The drive back from the festival was silent.

Haylee sat between Sam and David, her hand clasped tightly in Sam's. Josie lay curled at her feet, tense but quiet. The glow of celebration was long gone, replaced by the chill of something unspoken. They didn't need to say it aloud —Elliot had crossed a line.

Once they reached the campsite, Bertha was locked up tight, and they lit only a small fire, just enough for warmth. The stars above blinked indifferently down on them.

Sam finally broke the silence. "He came out of nowhere."

David leaned forward, elbows on knees. "Tell me exactly what happened."

Sam recounted the moment with precision—how Elliot emerged from the crowd, how his grip on Haylee wasn't just physical, it was... possessive. The way he looked at her—it wasn't about love, or even revenge. It was obsession.

"He was trying to take her," Sam said. "He wasn't just following. He was *waiting*."

Haylee shivered and pulled her jacket tighter. "I felt... paralyzed. Like something inside me recognized him before my mind did."

David stared into the fire. "That's how it starts. The veil between your world and his... it thins, and he presses through. But he's still not fully here. That's what scares me."

Sam nodded. "And he's getting stronger."

Haylee pulled the medallion from her pocket. "It's this. He's after this."

David didn't argue. "It's more than a symbol, more than a tracker. Elliot believes this is the key to unlocking everything. And if he gets it…"

"He'll become immortal," Haylee finished, her voice barely a whisper. "And fully materialize on this plane."

The fire crackled, throwing shadows across their faces.

David exhaled slowly. "Aggie must've used the medallion against him. Banished him somehow. That's why he's weak, why he hasn't already taken what he wants. But if he gets this back…"

"No firewall, no spell, no hiding," Sam muttered. "He wins."

Haylee looked between them. "So what do we do?"

David's gaze was steady. "We stay together. We outthink him. And when Riles gets here… we find a way to end this."

Sam reached over and squeezed Haylee's hand. "You're not alone in this."

She nodded, eyes shining—not with fear, but with fire.

For the first time, she wasn't just reacting. She was ready to fight.

Hometown Shadows

David was the one who brought it up the next morning. Over coffee and the last of the campfire toast, he folded the map in half and looked at them both. "I think we need to go back to Oregon for a bit," he said. "Home base. Just for a little while. Catch our breath. Recenter."

Haylee blinked. "You mean… back to *our* hometown?"

David nodded. "We need time to figure out what's next. And it wouldn't hurt to be somewhere familiar. Somewhere grounded."

It didn't take much convincing. A day later, they pulled into the town Haylee once thought she'd left behind for good. Bertha chugged up the final stretch of road like she was ready for a rest too.

She showed Sam her old street, the park she used to ride her bike through, the diner where she and her best friend used to split milkshakes. There was something comforting about being back—but also strange. The streets felt smaller. The memories, sharper.

They walked into a small shop Haylee used to love—a cozy mix of vintage books, candles, and handmade jewelry. The bell above the door chimed as they stepped in, Josie trotting alongside.

That's when it happened.

Jake.

He was standing by the front counter, of all places, chatting up the cashier like nothing had changed. His eyes found Haylee first. Then Sam. Then the way Sam casually placed his hand at the small of her back.

Jake's expression tightened.

"Well, look what the cat dragged in," he said, his voice coated in mock cheer.

Sam stiffened beside her. "Friend of yours?" he asked without looking away.

"Ex," Haylee muttered, already regretting coming inside.

Jake stepped forward. "Didn't think I'd see you again, Haylee. I figured once you ran off with your RV dreams, you'd forget where you came from."

"Still remember," she said coolly. "I just outgrew it."

Jake's smirk faltered. "And this guy?" He gestured to Sam. "Is he your... what, rebound?"

Before Haylee could respond, Sam took a step forward, his jaw set. "You've said enough."

Jake puffed up slightly, the way insecure men often did when they didn't know how to deal with being replaced.

"Sam," Haylee said sharply, stepping between them. "Don't. He's not worth it."

She turned to Jake, calm but firm. "We're just here for a few days. Don't make this harder than it needs to be."

Jake scoffed and backed off, muttering something under his breath as he returned to the counter.

They left the store in silence, the bell above the door chiming behind them again. Outside, Haylee exhaled.

"I'm sorry," she said. "I didn't know he'd be here."

Sam reached for her hand. "Don't be. He's the one who couldn't see what he had. I'm not him. And I'm not going anywhere."

Haylee looked up at him, her heart both heavy and full. "I know."

They walked on, Josie padding beside them, leaving the past where it belonged —behind them.

Old Contacts, New Shadows

While Haylee and Sam faced echoes of the past in town, David was thirty miles away, parked outside a modest roadside café just off the highway. His phone sat face-up on the table, untouched coffee cooling beside it. He was waiting.

The bell above the café door jingled. A man in a navy ball cap and leather jacket walked in, scanning the room until he spotted David. He slid into the seat across from him with a weary grunt.

"Damn, Dave. You always pick the scenic spots."

David gave a dry smile. "Appreciate you coming, Ray."

Ray leaned back and nodded. "You said it was urgent."

David didn't waste time. "You looked into that name I gave you—Elliot."

Ray's smirk faded. "Yeah. I did. You sure you wanna keep poking this hornet's nest?"

"I wouldn't have called if I wasn't."

Ray hesitated, then reached into his coat and slid a folded paper across the table. "I pulled some threads. A lot of dead ends. But the name's real. He's been off-grid for years—longer than most folks manage. A ghost. There's chatter about black projects, experimental tech, metaphysical interests. Fringe stuff. But here's the kicker—he was flagged once. Military intelligence. Then it got buried."

David frowned. "Buried by who?"

"That's the problem. I don't know. But it was deliberate. Someone didn't want him on record. Not in any obvious way."

David absorbed the information. "Could he be connected to something… otherworldly?"

Ray paused, then nodded slowly. "Wouldn't be the first time someone tried to transcend the rules of physics. But this guy? He didn't just dabble. He believed."

David leaned forward. "What do you mean?"

"I mean Elliot wasn't chasing power for power's sake. He thought he could become more than human. Immortal, maybe. And from what little I could find... he wasn't working alone."

David stiffened. "You're saying there are others?"

Ray shrugged. "There were. Maybe still are. Cult-like circles. Quiet, careful. But if Elliot's resurfacing... you're gonna want more than a flashlight and good intentions."

David's jaw clenched. He stood, leaving a few bills on the table. "Thanks, Ray."

"Be careful, Dave. Some doors don't close once they've been opened."

David didn't answer. As he stepped outside into the wind, his mind was already racing. Haylee had to know. They all did.

Back Where It Began

David returned just before dusk, the sun casting long golden shadows across the modest cul-de-sac. His truck rumbled into the driveway beside Bertha, tires crunching over gravel. Haylee was sitting on the porch steps with Josie curled at her feet and Bella nestled beside her like a guardian.

Sam stepped out from the RV as David climbed out. One look told them both everything: his face was tight, his eyes worn. Something about the conversation he'd had hadn't sat well.

"Find anything?" Haylee asked, standing.

David nodded once, slowly. "Yeah. Enough to keep me up tonight."

They all went inside—familiar walls and worn-in furniture welcoming them like old friends. The kettle whistled soon after, and Haylee busied herself making tea while Sam and David sat down at the kitchen table.

David glanced at them both, then began. "My buddy Ray dug deeper into Elliot. What he found doesn't make sense—official records vanish, weird mentions of classified projects, rumors about cult behavior. And here's the kicker: Elliot believed in something... metaphysical. Not just power. Transcendence."

Haylee sat down slowly, hands wrapped around her mug. "He really thinks he can become something... more."

"Maybe even immortal," David confirmed grimly.

The silence that followed wasn't heavy—it was thoughtful. Everyone was trying to stitch meaning out of the tangle.

Josie gave a low whine, as if even she could feel the weight in the room. Haylee finally spoke. "I don't know what we're walking into. But I think we're getting closer. And I want to be ready."

David met her gaze. "We'll make sure of it."

The warmth of the house, the clink of mugs, the rhythmic thump of Bella's tail against the floor—it was a fragile peace, but it was theirs for the night. And in that quiet space between danger and discovery, they rested.

Chapter Twenty:
New Roads, Old Shadows

David stepped onto the back porch with his phone pressed to his ear. The late afternoon sun filtered through the pine trees, casting long shadows across the yard. He'd finally gotten a call back from Riles.

"Didn't think I'd hear from you so soon." David smirked faintly.

"Yeah, well... figured it was time to check if you were still breathing." Riles replied. "This trail's colder than I'd like, but it's not dead yet," he replied, his voice gravelly.

David glanced through the kitchen window where Haylee and Sam were cleaning up from breakfast. "We're in Oregon now. Took a breather. Regrouping. You sound like you could use one too."

Riles sighed. "That obvious, huh?"

David nodded to himself. "Ray—my Navy buddy—found something. Elliot isn't just a ghost from the past. His trail goes deeper than we thought. High-level projects, rumors about metaphysical experiments, and people who've gone missing after asking too many questions."

There was silence on the line.

Then: "Yeah... I believe it," Riles muttered. "I'll head your way. Text me the address, should be there by tomorrow morning."

David ended the call and stepped back inside.

Meanwhile, Haylee and Sam were loading up Bertha for a short trip to nearby **Happy Pines Campground**.

David's house was cozy, but Haylee had suggested they give everyone some space. Besides, she and Sam needed time to breathe. Alone.

"Call me if Riles shows up sooner," Haylee said, giving her dad a hug.
"Will do. You two be careful."

Josie bounded up into the RV as if she knew they were heading out, and Bella
was already curled in her spot on the dash. As Bertha rumbled to life, David
watched them pull away with a strange mixture of worry and relief.

They had space. For now.

Four Souls, One Quiet Night

The winding road to Happy Pines Campground offered a welcome change from the weight of recent revelations. Tucked beneath a canopy of old pines and nestled against a glimmering lake, the campground exhaled a familiar serenity that Haylee didn't know she needed—until she felt it.

Bertha groaned softly as Sam eased her into a shaded spot near the edge of the grounds. There were only a few other campers parked far enough away to offer a sense of privacy, and the scent of cedar clung to the cool air.

Josie bounded out first, nose twitching with every new woodland smell. Bella, ever the queen, leapt gracefully onto the dash and stretched like she owned the whole campground.

Haylee and Sam worked in quiet sync, setting up camp like seasoned travelers. It didn't take long—Bertha was home now, and they knew every creak and quirk of her. Sam started a small fire while Haylee laid out a blanket nearby. The sun filtered through the trees in warm streaks, casting dappled light over everything like a gentle reminder that peace could still exist, even now.

"Feels like coming full circle," Haylee said, looking around with a soft smile. "This place… it's where everything started." Haylee said, dropping onto the blanket beside Josie, who had promptly collapsed in the grass with a satisfied sigh.

Sam smiled, setting the kettle over the fire. "It's definitely beautiful."

As the water began to bubble, Bella prowled along the picnic table, tail flicking with curiosity. She batted at a pinecone, knocking it to the ground with regal disdain.

They didn't talk much that evening. They didn't need to. A quiet understanding passed between them with every shared look, every subtle touch of a hand. They were healing—not just from what they'd learned, but from what they'd carried long before they met each other.

Under Familiar Stars

That evening, the campground was quiet, cloaked in the hush of pine trees and the steady hum of cicadas. The fire crackled gently, casting golden light across Bertha's weathered side. Haylee and Sam sat in the glow, Josie snoozing nearby and Bella curled contentedly in her favorite patch of the dashboard.

Haylee leaned into Sam's side, a blanket wrapped around both of them. "It's strange being back here," she murmured. "Like I never really left, but I'm someone else entirely."

Sam smiled. "Maybe that's the magic of coming back—you bring all the new pieces of yourself to the place where you started."

She looked up at him, eyes reflecting the flicker of the flames. "You always know what to say."

He reached into his jacket pocket and pulled out a small, worn box. "I've had this for a while," he said, almost sheepishly. "Picked it up in a shop before everything went… sideways. I didn't know when would be the right time to give it to you, but—tonight felt like it."

He opened the box and revealed a delicate silver locket. Inside was a tiny compass etched into one side, and on the other, a blank space, waiting for whatever memory she chose to tuck inside.

Haylee touched it gently, then looked at him. "It's beautiful."

"You've always been the compass," Sam said. "Even when you didn't know it." She leaned forward and kissed him, slow and certain. The kiss deepened, unfolding into something quiet and intimate. No rush. No fear. Just warmth between them, safe and still beneath the stars. The world would always have chaos—but tonight, in this familiar place, they had peace.

And each other.

That night, for the first time in days, maybe weeks, the four of them slept soundly—together, safe, and still.

Old Friends and New Beginnings

Haylee and Sam had fallen asleep outside, wrapped in each other's arms beneath the stars, Josie snoring quietly at their feet, and Bella curled beside them like a furry comma in the night.

Morning crept in slowly—golden light filtering through the tall pines. The peaceful stillness was broken by the low rumble of an approaching engine. Haylee stirred first, blinking against the light. Sam grumbled and shifted behind her.

The sound grew louder until a familiar golf cart rolled to a stop nearby, kicking up a puff of dust and a cheerful voice rang out. "Well, I'll be damned. Is that Bertha?"

Haylee sat up, startled, and broke into a grin. "Marla?"

Marla and Benny, two of the kindest and quirkiest nomads Haylee had met early in her journey, climbed out of their rig with matching grins. They looked exactly the same—sun-kissed, windblown, and radiating joy.

Sam scrambled upright beside Haylee, both of them adjusting clothes and smoothing hair like teenagers caught making out in the back of someone's parents' car. Josie barked excitedly and darted toward the couple.

"Oh my stars, it *is* you!" Marla called out, laughing as she bent to scratch Josie behind the ears. "You're back, girl! And… you brought company?"

Haylee blushed, her smile wide. "This is Sam."

Sam stood and extended a hand. "Nice to meet you both."

"Sam, huh?" Benny grinned. "Glad to see someone's brave enough to ride shotgun with this one. She's got fire."

"Don't I know it," Sam replied with a wink.

Marla took Haylee's hands. "We've missed you around here. Your energy's been hard to replace. You sticking around for the big New Year's bash tonight?"

Haylee exchanged a glance with Sam. "There's a party?"

"Oh honey, this campground turns into a lantern-lit wonderland. Bonfires, live music, the works. You, your guy, your pup—and whoever else you've got—are absolutely coming."

Haylee laughed. "We'd love to. My dad's coming by later too."

"Oh good! It'll be great to meet him. Anyone else?"

Haylee hesitated for half a second. "A friend of ours—Riles, maybe."

Benny raised an eyebrow playfully. "The more the merrier."

Marla clapped her hands. "Perfect! I'll save you all a spot by the fire. Don't be late!"

As Marla and Benny headed back to their golf cart to finish setting up, Haylee leaned into Sam's side and whispered, "I forgot how good this place feels."

He kissed her temple. "Then let's make some new memories."

Dust and Arrival

Riles pulled up to David's house just before noon, his Jeep trailing a storm of dust behind it. He looked like he hadn't slept in days—clothes rumpled, eyes shadowed with exhaustion, and tension clinging to every movement.

David stepped onto the porch, arms crossed. "You look like hell."

Riles huffed out a tired laugh. "I feel worse. Got anything stronger than a welcome mat?"

"I've got hot water and a clean bed. Pick one."

"Both. In that order."

David handed him a towel and gestured toward the guest room. "Shower's down the hall. You can crash in there after."

Riles didn't argue. After a muttered thanks, he disappeared inside.

While Riles got settled, David stepped outside and called Haylee. She answered on the second ring.

"He made it," David said. "Looks like he drove straight through the night."

"Good," Haylee replied. "Let him rest. There's a New Year's Eve celebration here at Happy Pines tonight. You both should come."

David glanced toward the house. "We'll be there after he gets some sleep. I think he could use a reminder that the world isn't all shadows and bad news."

Haylee smiled softly. "We all could."

Pieces of the Present

After breakfast and a quick tidy-up around the site, Haylee and Sam decided to drive into town to pick up a few things for the New Year's celebration. With Josie and Bella safely curled up in the RV's coziest corners, the two of them set out, hand in hand, ready for a quiet day together.

They wandered through the small town's streets, popping into local shops that bustled with holiday leftovers and new year anticipation. Strings of lights still hung lazily from the storefronts, and the scent of pine and cinnamon lingered in the air.

In one of the quaint little shops, Haylee paused at a display of frames and keepsakes. A quiet idea lit in her eyes.

"Mind if I duck in here for a second?" she asked.

Sam smiled. "I'll grab us a couple of drinks from the bakery across the street."

Inside, Haylee browsed through shelves until she found the small self-service photo kiosk tucked in the back corner. Pulling out her phone, she selected a photo taken just a few days ago—one where she and Sam were standing in front of Bertha, laughing, arms around each other, Josie sitting loyally at their feet and Bella curled up in the window behind them, peeking out with regal indifference. It was candid and real, a snapshot of the life they had built—chaotic, magical, and filled with love.

She printed the photo, then carefully trimmed it to size. It fit perfectly inside the locket Sam had given her. She clicked it shut with a soft smile.

Outside, Sam returned just as she stepped out of the shop.

"Mission accomplished?" he asked, handing her a warm cup of spiced cider.

"Definitely," Haylee said, slipping her hand into his. "Let's get back. I think tonight might be kind of magical."

Sam grinned, wrapping an arm around her shoulders. "With you? It always is."

Chapter Twenty-One:
By Firelight and Lanterns

The campground at Happy Pines buzzed with excitement. Strings of soft golden lights twinkled between the tall pines, casting a warm glow over the winding gravel paths. Children chased each other with glow sticks, couples wandered hand in hand, and campfires crackled in nearly every direction. It was New Year's Eve, and the community had come alive.

Haylee stood outside Bertha, smoothing down her sweater as she looked around at the magic unfolding. Josie had a festive bandana tied around her neck, and Bella, thoroughly unimpressed, sat on the dashboard, watching from the window like a dignified queen surveying her kingdom.

Sam stepped out behind her, carrying a tray of hot cider. "This feels like something out of a dream," he said, offering her a mug.

"It really does," Haylee agreed, sipping. "And we deserve this. Just for one night, to breathe."

They wandered toward the large communal fire pit, where Marla and Benny waved them over to their saved seats. Folding chairs circled the bonfire, and someone had set up a makeshift stage nearby where a guitarist strummed softly, drawing in an easy crowd.

"Still waiting on your dad and friend?" Marla asked as they settled in.

"Should be here soon," Sam replied, glancing toward the road.

Haylee smiled, her heart light. For the first time in weeks, the weight of the unknown didn't feel quite so crushing. Tonight was about celebration. Tomorrow, they'd face whatever came next—together.

Karaoke and Keepsakes

Riles blinked himself awake to the smell of coffee and the sound of David moving around the kitchen. He swung his legs off the guest bed with a grunt just as David peeked in, mug in hand.

"Feel like a party?" David asked, raising a brow.

Riles chuckled, voice gravelly. "Sure, why not? I've got one clean shirt left and a reputation for bad dancing to uphold."

Not long after, the two men climbed into David's truck and drove toward Happy Pines. As the sun slanted through the trees, painting golden stripes across the winding road. When they pulled into the campground, Bertha stood like a familiar sentinel, nestled in her usual cozy spot.

Haylee and Sam were already set up near the fire ring, folding chairs arranged in a semicircle with Josie sprawled out in the middle like she owned the place. Bella was tucked into Sam's flannel shirt, purring softly.

Haylee waved as they approached. "Hey! You made it!"

David greeted them with a warm grin, but it was Riles who paused, his eyes scanning the scene. Something about it—the firelight, the comfort, the laughter—made his shoulders relax for the first time in weeks.

Introductions were swift and easy. Marla and Benny joined them a few minutes later with s'mores supplies and stories, welcoming Riles without hesitation. "Any friend of Haylee's is family," Marla insisted.

Laughter carried through the trees as someone wheeled out a beat-up karaoke machine and a mic. The singing was spontaneous and chaotic—but joyful. When Sam nudged Haylee and whispered, "Come on, we've gotta do this," she rolled her eyes but smiled.

They stood together, awkward at first, until the opening notes of "Stuck in the Middle with You" played. The crowd cheered.

Haylee and Sam sang—badly, playfully, in tune only when it didn't matter. David laughed until his face hurt, and even Riles cracked a real smile.

Later, after the applause and gentle teasing had faded into the background, Haylee took Sam's hand and led him away from the group. The stars stretched above them, crisp and clear.

"I got something for this," she said softly, pulling out the locket from beneath her sweater and opening it.

Inside was the small photo of the four of them—Sam, Haylee, Josie, and Bella.

Sam looked at it, then back at her.

"It's perfect," he said.

And in that quiet moment, with firelight flickering behind them and laughter echoing softly in the distance, everything else faded away.

Midnight and a Warning

As midnight approached, the campground came alive with laughter, and the soft hum of music drifting from someone's portable speaker. Children ran around with sparklers waving in the air, and couples snuggled under blankets by the fire. Haylee, Sam, David, and Riles had claimed a cozy corner near the main gathering, sipping cider and watching the stars blink into view.

Marla handed out sparklers with uncontained glee, Benny manned the bonfire like a seasoned conductor of warmth. Josie lay between Haylee and Sam, occasionally lifting her head to sniff the air. Bella had found her perch on a blanket David laid out, curled up and purring beneath the firelight's glow.

"Five... four... three... two... one!"

Cheers erupted. Fireworks shot into the sky in a burst of color. Haylee turned toward Sam, her cheeks flushed with joy. He cupped her face gently, and their lips met in a soft, lingering kiss that said everything they couldn't in words. They pulled apart with shared laughter and forehead pressed to forehead, anchoring themselves in each other as the world turned the page on a new year.

Then... it happened.

Just after midnight, the air changed.

It was subtle at first—an almost imperceptible drop in temperature, a hush that settled over the trees. Benny looked up from the fire. "Storm rolling in?" he asked, his voice uncertain.

Haylee stiffened. "That's not weather," she murmured.

Sam's hand found hers instantly. David and Riles exchanged a look that needed no explanation. They all felt it—a ripple in the atmosphere, a warning carried on the breeze.

Marla and the other campers didn't notice, too lost in celebration. But the quartet by the fire knew better.

It wasn't thunder that loomed. It was a different kind of storm.

Without needing to say it, they knew the night was over. Haylee and Sam packed up quietly, Josie already running towards the RV. Bella leapt in with feline grace. David and Riles nodded their goodbyes, heading back toward David's house with quiet resolve.

No dramatic farewell. No drawn-out discussions. Just a silent agreement to give space for the moment—and to prepare for what was coming.

Haylee curled beside Sam in the RV bed, watching shadows flicker on the ceiling. He wrapped his arms around her, and for now, that was enough.

A new year had begun. But peace was fleeting.

And the road ahead would demand everything they had left to give.

Chapter Twenty-Two:
Restless Roads and Familiar Faces

The first couple of days after the New Year had passed in a quiet blur. The celebration at Happy Pines left a warm afterglow, but Haylee couldn't shake the sense that they were standing still for too long.

She needed motion. The open road. Something new on the horizon.

Over coffee and a quiet breakfast under Bertha's awning, she finally said it out loud. "I think I need to move again. I don't like sitting still too long."
Sam gave a small smile. "I've been thinking the same thing."

David, leaning against a picnic table with his mug in hand, nodded slowly. "It might be good for you two to hit the road for a bit. Riles and I are going to keep digging—Ray's still feeding us bits and pieces, but we need time to lay it all out."

Sam perked up. "Actually... my sister lives up near the Washington coast. She and her wife just had a baby, and they've been asking me to visit for months. Might be a good place to go. Some normalcy."

Haylee smiled softly, remembering the way Sam had once mentioned his sister in passing. "You think she'll be okay with us showing up out of the blue?"

Sam nodded. "She's been wanting me to visit for ages. I think she'll love you—and Josie and Bella too."

David set his mug down. "Might be the breather you both need. I'll check in with you when Riles and I know more. We'll handle the heavy lifting for a bit."

Haylee looked at Sam, then at the familiar campground where she'd started it all. "Yeah," she said softly. "Let's go make some new memories."

Between the Lines of Quiet Roads

Haylee and Sam stood outside Bertha, the morning air still cool as the sun climbed slowly over the pines. Steam curled from their travel mugs as they sipped the last of their coffee. The laughter and warmth of New Year's Eve already felt like it had happened weeks ago.

Haylee exhaled, watching the mist of her breath fade. "I think it's time."

Sam nodded. "Yeah. Road's calling again."

David leaned against his truck nearby, arms crossed loosely, a knowing look on his face. "You two sure you don't want to wait a bit longer?"

Haylee smiled. "If I stay still much longer, I might take root."

Riles, still half-asleep and clutching a thermos, added, "Can't say I blame you. Waiting around feels like walking on broken glass."

Sam clapped David on the shoulder. "We won't be far, but far enough."

David raised an eyebrow. "She know you're bringing company?"

Sam chuckled and pulled out his phone. "Just texted her."

Kate's reply came quickly, glowing on the screen:

Finally! Can't wait. I'll spruce up the guest room for you two! Safe travels, little bro.

Haylee peered over his arm and smiled. "She sounds excited."

"She'll love you," Sam said.

They packed up quickly. Josie hopped into the passenger seat like she already knew the plan. Bella, ever aloof, took her spot in the kitchen sink with a yawn.

Riles and David stood by as the RV rumbled to life.

"Don't do anything stupid until we meet again," Riles said.

"No promises," Sam called out with a grin.

Haylee leaned out the window. "Let us know if Ray turns up anything new. We'll be back when it counts."

David offered a quiet wave. "Take care of each other."

And just like that, Bertha rolled out of Happy Pines, back onto the open road, away from the ghosts of the last few weeks. For now, there were no texts, no trackers, no shadows.

Just the hum of tires on asphalt, the rustle of maps, and the promise of a quiet stretch of road leading north.

They didn't speak for a while. They didn't have to. They just breathed.

Together.

Detours & Dog Hair

Halfway to Washington, the journey started to feel less like an escape and more like what it was meant to be: a reprieve.

The first laugh of the day came when Josie, freshly soaked from a surprise creek dip, bounded into Bertha and shook herself dry—right next to Sam's freshly unwrapped sandwich.

Haylee doubled over laughing as Sam held the soggy bread at arm's length. "Guess I'm having Josie-flavored turkey now."

"She just wanted to share lunch," Haylee teased.

They pulled into a small town with a name neither of them could pronounce and stumbled across a diner with a painted wooden sign that read: *Griddle Me This*.

Inside, the air smelled like syrup and nostalgia. The owner, a woman in her sixties with bright red glasses and a louder laugh, insisted they try the house specialty: peanut butter banana pancakes with cinnamon whipped cream.

"It sounds like chaos," Sam whispered.

"Exactly our vibe," Haylee whispered back.

Josie got her own slice of bacon, and Bella received a saucer of milk that she sniffed at once before glaring judgmentally at the fluorescent lighting.
Back on the road, Bertha hummed along like she was enjoying herself, too.
That is, until Bella knocked over a small stack of books Sam had carefully arranged to read later. He turned just in time to trip over them.

"Seriously? This cat is trying to sabotage me," he muttered.

Haylee giggled from the driver's seat. "You should know better than to try to organize anything in her domain."

The moment passed into another, and then another—small joys stringing together like fairy lights, lighting the way through whatever came next.

They didn't know what they'd find in Washington, but for now, the road was theirs.

And it was enough.

Chapter Twenty-Three:
Salt Air and Open Arms

Bertha rumbled down the quiet lane that led to Kate's beach house—perched just above the rocky shoreline of the Washington coast. Gray mist curled over the dunes, the sea air cool and briny, the wind carrying the scent of driftwood and pine.

Haylee leaned forward in her seat as the quaint cottage came into view. "That's it?" she whispered, awestruck. The house wasn't massive, but it radiated warmth—big picture windows facing the water, a wraparound porch, and a hammock swinging lazily between two old cedar posts.

"She's always had a thing for hidden gems," Sam said, pulling into the gravel driveway.

Before Bertha came to a full stop, the front door flung open and Kate came bounding down the steps. Her wild curls bounced as she sprinted across the yard and flung open the RV door.

"Sam!" she shrieked, throwing her arms around him in a hug so fierce it knocked the breath from his lungs.

"You'd think I'd been lost at sea," he wheezed.

Haylee stepped down slowly, smiling as she took in the scene. Josie bolted from behind her and made a beeline for the open yard—bounding through the damp grass and circling the porch with excitement.

Behind Kate, a petite woman with cropped black hair—Meg—emerged from the house, a baby girl on her hip. The little one squealed and clapped her chubby hands at the sight of the dog.

"Well hello," Meg called with a laugh. "That must be Josie."

Sam turned to Haylee, gesturing proudly. "Haylee, meet my sister Kate, her wife Meg, and the adorable hurricane of a child is Lydia."

"Hey there," Haylee said, offering a warm handshake.

Kate pulled her into a hug instead. "You're real. I'm so glad. We've heard nothing but glowing reports."

"I promise I haven't exaggerated too much," Sam said, smirking.

As Josie made fast friends with Lydia—circling her protectively while the baby reached for her fur—Bella peeked out from one of Bertha's windows with a regal air, unimpressed.

"She can come in when she's ready," Meg said, spotting the cat. "We've got a sunroom she'll probably claim by dinnertime."

Haylee exhaled deeply, tension leaving her shoulders for the first time in weeks. Something about this place—the waves, the warmth, the welcoming chaos— already felt like a balm.

And for the first time in a while, they weren't just visitors.

They were home. For now.

Echoes Across the Line

Later that evening, once they were parked along the beach just outside Kate's, Haylee stepped out of Bertha to call David. The sun dipped low over the horizon, casting golden light across the sand.

David answered on the second ring. "You make it okay?"

"Yeah, we're here. Kate and Meg were waiting for us with open arms—and a baby who immediately adopted Josie."

David chuckled. "Sounds like a good start. I'm glad you're safe. Listen, Ray found something… a back door into Elliot's world. There's a group—people who seem invested in helping him return. We don't know who they are yet, but it's organized."

Haylee's chest tightened. "Of course it is."

"Ray thinks they're helping from this side. Trying to bridge the gap while Elliot is limited."

Haylee nodded slowly, letting the wind carry her thoughts. "We told Kate and Meg a little. Not everything, just enough to be honest… without dragging them into the middle of it."

"Smart move. Keep it light."

"Kate offered to let us park Bertha in a private garage. Said we could stay at the house until we leave."

"Good. You need the rest. Just stay alert."

"Always."

They ended the call, and Haylee turned back toward the beach house where laughter spilled out from inside.

For now, it was enough to be surrounded by warmth, while the cold truth of the world outside waited for its next move.

She wasn't running. Not anymore. But she would be ready. Whatever came next.

Quiet Warnings

Back in Oregon, dusk had settled like a soft shroud over David's quiet house. The kitchen light buzzed faintly as Riles leaned against the counter, arms crossed, watching David pace with a glass of water in hand.

"He said there's more than whispers now," David muttered. "There's organization. Money. Some kind of underground network that believes in what Elliot's trying to do."

Riles exhaled, rubbing a hand down his face. "Believes—or fears him enough to help. Either way, they're working from this side. Setting the stage."

David sat down at the table with a weary sigh. "Ray called them sympathizers. Said they're planting breadcrumbs—signs for him to follow, or maybe signals for him to return."

Riles nodded slowly. "Makes sense. Elliot's limited on the physical plane, but if enough people open doors for him... he won't need to cross over on his own."

There was a long pause. The weight of it all hung between them.

David finally broke the silence. "She's too far away."

"She's not alone," Riles said firmly, meeting his gaze. "Sam's with her. And that girl? She's not the same scared woman I met a month ago. She's sharper now. Stronger."

David's jaw tightened. "Still doesn't mean I sleep any easier."

"No. But it means we've still got a fighting chance."

A distant howl of wind rattled the windows. Riles glanced toward the front door.

"I don't like standing still either," he admitted. "But we can do more from here right now. We're in Ray's backyard. Let's use it."

David gave a slow nod. "Tomorrow. We dig deeper."

And as the night deepened, neither of them said what they were really thinking —that whatever this group was planning, it wouldn't be long before Elliot made his next move.

Thin Walls, Long Shadows

David sat at his kitchen table, a mug of coffee cooling beside a stack of printouts. Riles stood near the window, arms crossed, watching the street like it might whisper secrets if he stared long enough.

"Still nothing concrete," Riles muttered. "But something's not right. Ray's got a trail—files, logs, case reports—but they're all half-gone. Like someone got there first."

David sighed, rubbing his temples. "Missing records, deleted emails, fragmented hard drives. I've seen this pattern before. Someone's covering tracks."

"Ray called it a pattern of reactivations," Riles said. "Old names popping up, dormant files pinged again. It's like they're rallying."

David's expression hardened. "And you think it's Elliot's people."

Riles nodded. "Or people who believe in him. Either way, they're helping from this side."

Outside, wind shook the pine branches. David reached for his phone, then stopped. "We can't tell Haylee. Not yet. Not unless we know more."

Riles turned to look at him. "You really think she's in danger right now?"

David was quiet. Then he said, low, "She's never not been."

Meanwhile, back in Washington, Bella sat perched on the RV dashboard. Her golden eyes fixed on the window. For a moment, her fur rose.

Then the moment passed.

The Edge of Knowing

Haylee sat with Meg on the back deck of the beach house, wrapped in a knit blanket. Lydia was napping, Kate was prepping dinner, and the sea stretched endlessly before them.

"Aggie left me a map I still can't read," Haylee said softly. "And dreams I can't explain."

Meg nodded, listening without judgment. "I believe in dreams," she said. "They carry more than we think."

Haylee hesitated. "You ever dream about someone you've never met… and still know their name?"

Meg's brow furrowed. Then she said, almost shyly, "I have one dream that repeats. A forest. Burning trees. And a man with silver eyes standing just beyond the flames. I never see him clearly, but I always wake up cold." Haylee's mouth went dry. That matched her own dreams—too closely. "When did it start?" she asked.

"A year ago. Around the time Lydia was born."

Haylee felt something stir in her chest. The Veil. Maybe it wasn't just thinning around her.

She glanced back toward Bertha. Toward Bella. Toward Josie curled near the fire pit.

Meg watched her carefully. "Haylee… he's reaching, isn't he?"

Haylee nodded once. "But we're not going to let him through."

An Omen on the Wind

That night, after the house quieted and the stars painted silver streaks across the sky, Haylee and Sam took a walk along the shoreline. Josie bounded ahead, barking at the waves.

As they turned up the gravel path toward the garage, they both stopped.

A low, throaty growl broke the silence—Bella. She stood planted at the edge of the garage, her fur puffed and her gaze locked on the door.

Haylee quickened her step. "Bella?"

The garage door creaked open slightly, just enough for a whisper of night air to escape.

Sam stepped ahead of Haylee and reached for the door handle.

Inside, nestled at the seam of the threshold, was a single feather—black, long, and faintly shimmering in the moonlight.

Bella leapt, pawing at it.

Haylee bent down, gently lifting the feather before Bella could reach it. As her fingers touched it, a shock of cold raced through her arm.

Sam touched her shoulder. "What is it?"

Haylee swallowed. "He's reaching for us. Even from wherever he is… he's trying to get through."

Sam took the feather and walked it over to the fire pit. He tossed it in. It hissed and twisted once before turning to smoke.

Bella, now calm, curled beside the pit. The wind kept blowing.

And the night held its breath.

Chapter Twenty-Four:
The Man in the Amber Coat

His desk lamp flickered once, a soft pulse of unease humming in the corners of his small apartment. He had a corkboard pinned with scribbled notes and photographs—some dating back decades, others mere days old. Elliot's face was absent, but his shadow touched every corner.

A knock at the door. Sharp. Deliberate.

Ray wasn't expecting company.

Ray approached with caution, hand hovering near the drawer that held his sidearm. He looked through the peephole.

A man in a long amber-colored coat stood waiting. Wide-brimmed hat. Gray scarf. Hands gloved. Not a stranger—but not someone Ray could place.

He opened the door a crack.

"Can I help you?"

The man smiled, too polite. "Ray Becker? I've been following your research. Brilliant work. May I come in?"

Ray stiffened. "Who are you?"

"Someone who appreciates forgotten truths. I go by Ezra. Just Ezra."

The man stepped forward before being invited. Ray, reluctantly, let him in.

Ezra glanced around the cluttered room. "You've come close to understanding the pattern. Most don't make it this far before they're... redirected."

Ray frowned. "Redirected by who?"

Ezra smiled again, slow and unsettling. "By forces who prefer Elliot remain a story, not a warning."

Ray tensed. "So you are with him."

Ezra shrugged. "I serve a vision. Elliot merely helps shape it."

"Why are you here?"

Ezra leaned closer, eyes gleaming. "To tell you that doors are opening. Some can't be closed. And those on the wrong side of truth often suffer for their curiosity."

Ray didn't flinch. "Then I guess I'm already damned."

Ezra's grin widened. "We all are. Some just wear it better."

He turned, his coat brushing the floor. Before Ray could move, Ezra opened the door and stepped out into the hall. When Ray rushed after him—nothing. Just silence.

Ray shut the door. Locked it. Then picked up his phone.

Time to call David.

The Warning

David answered on the third ring, his voice tight with concern. "Ray? Everything alright?"

"No. We've got a problem," Ray said. "I had a visitor tonight. He called himself Ezra. Wore an amber coat. Knew too much."

Riles leaned in from the couch, catching David's expression shift. David put the call on speaker.

"He knew what I've been working on," Ray continued. "Mentioned Elliot by name. Claimed he's not the only one helping him—that there are others, maybe a whole group, working to reopen something."

Riles muttered, "Hell."

David stayed quiet a moment, absorbing it. "Did he say what they want?"

"Power. Access. He said doors are opening. I don't know what that means yet, but it's not good. He threatened me, indirectly. Just enough to let me know I'm on borrowed time."

"Did he leave anything behind? A card, a symbol?"

Ray hesitated. "A black feather. Left it at my door."

David felt his stomach knot.

"We're not just being watched," Ray continued. "They're moving. And they're not waiting for Elliot to get stronger. They're already building something." David exhaled. "Then we better prepare faster."

Ray lowered his voice. "He wasn't rattled. Calm. That kind of calm that comes from being untouchable. This wasn't a warning. It was a prelude."

David nodded slowly, even though Ray couldn't see him. "We need to tighten our net. Keep this between us for now. Haylee and Sam are okay, last I heard. In Washington. Let them breathe."

Riles crossed his arms. "But not for long. Because if this Ezra shows up again —we won't have time to play catch-up."

"Agreed," David said. "Thanks, Ray. Lock everything down. And keep that feather. Might come in handy."

"Will do," Ray replied.

As the call ended, David and Riles sat in silence, the weight of what they'd just heard settling like a fog.

Ezra was real. And he wasn't alone.

David looked at Riles. "We need to bring Haylee and Sam up to speed soon. But not yet. Not until we know how far this goes."

Riles gave a tight nod. "Then let's find out."

The pages on the table suddenly felt heavier.

The war hadn't started yet.

But the first soldier had just knocked on their door.

Echoes on the Breeze

Back at the beach house in Washington, the evening air had grown crisp. Haylee and Sam walked hand in hand along the edge of the bluff, Bella padding a few paces ahead, tail flicking. Josie was playing in the sand.

They reached the porch, the scent of ocean salt giving way to something faintly metallic.

Bella stopped short. Her fur bristled.

A growl rumbled from her throat as she turned toward the porch door. "That wasn't like that before," Sam said, pulling Haylee slightly behind him.

Bella darted toward the door and began pawing at something wedged in the gap. Another long, black feather.

Haylee knelt down beside her. "Same kind as before..."

They exchanged a look. Sam retrieved the feather, holding it up to the waning light. "We can't keep pretending this is a coincidence."

Haylee took a deep breath. "We need to call Dad."

They sat in the adirondack chairs on the porch, Sam put the call on speaker.

"Hey," David answered. "Everything alright?"

"Not exactly," Sam said. "We found another feather. In the porch door."

Riles' voice cut in. "Another one?"

Sam hesitated. "Yeah, we found one in the RV door last night."

Riles' suspicions growing. "Where are they?"

"Well...Sam said reluctantly. We burned the first one, but kept this one."

David swore under his breath. "You burned it?"

"Why?" Haylee asked, her brow creased.

David exchanged a look with Riles. "We don't know what kind of marker it is. It could be a tether. Or a warning. Burning it might've broken something... or triggered something."

"Great," Sam muttered. "Well, too late now."

A sigh from David. "Ray found one too. And he had a visitor. Called himself Ezra."

"And we just learned he might be part of a larger group. People helping Elliot from this side."

Haylee crossed her arms. "We need to know more."

Riles replied, "We're working on it. Just... stay close. And keep that cat nearby. She seems to know more than she lets on."

They ended the call with a shared silence. Outside, the breeze picked up. And the porch door creaked again.

Unseen eyes were watching.

Eyes in the Crowd

The next morning, Haylee and Sam joined Kate, Meg, and baby Lydia for a day trip into the nearby coastal town. They strolled through quiet streets decorated with string lights and winter wreaths, the crisp ocean breeze wrapping around them like a memory.

Haylee was laughing with Meg about a bottle of wine they picked up at the local shop when Sam suddenly slowed.

Someone was watching them.

A man leaned casually against a lamppost near the corner of the bookstore. Long coat. Hood low over his face. He wasn't shopping. Wasn't moving. Just standing there.

Sam's eyes narrowed. He kept walking but subtly shifted his position to keep the man in view.

Haylee noticed his change in energy. "What's up?"

"Nothing. Just... keeping an eye out."

In the glass of a nearby antique store window, Haylee caught a glimpse of someone behind them. When she turned—no one was there. Just the reflection of the street and the fog starting to roll in.

She tried to shake it off, but something about the moment unsettled her.

Kate, sensing the change, picked up Lydia and said, "Maybe we should head back. Looks like the weather's turning." No one argued.

As they walked back to the car, Haylee glanced over her shoulder.

The man was gone.

But the unease lingered.

Whispers on the Page

The soft scratching of pen against paper was the only sound in the RV as Haylee sat cross-legged on the bed, Bella curled near her feet and Josie dozing by the door.

January 14th, 2025

I can't sleep again.

We're here at Sam's sister's beach house — and it's perfect. Calm. Warm, even with the chill in the air. Lydia's giggle somehow manages to soothe my nerves better than any deep breath ever could.

But something's... shifting.

There was another feather. This one at the porch door. Bella saw it before we did — growling like she could sense something beyond what we can see.

We called my dad and Riles. Turns out Ray got one too. And a visitor. A man named Ezra. He didn't say much, but he left a mark — and not just with the feather.

I hate feeling watched. We had a run-in in town today. Sam noticed it first — a guy standing too still. Too quiet. I caught a glimpse in a reflection, and by the time I turned around, he was gone.

Gone. But the feeling wasn't.

We now know that Elliot has people helping him — and that somehow I'm in the center of this thing.

But what else I know:

Sam makes me feel safe.

Kate and Meg welcomed me without question.

And for now — just for tonight — we're okay.

Tomorrow might be different.

Tomorrow probably will be different.

But tonight, I'll breathe in the ocean air and listen to Bella's quiet purring and remind myself that I'm not alone.

Not anymore.

Chapter Twenty-five:
Where the Veil Thins

The night air was quiet outside the beach house, the waves a low hush in the distance. Inside the guest room, Haylee stirred beneath the quilt, a bead of sweat trickling down her temple despite the coolness of the January evening.

Her dream had started like the others—fog, water, a blurred figure in the distance. But this time, Aggie came into focus faster than before, walking toward her through a shifting mist.

"Haylee," she said, her voice clear and close, as if she were standing right next to the bed. "You're stronger than you know. You must stay grounded. Look to Bertha—she still holds answers."

Haylee tried to reach out, but the scene shifted sharply.

Elliot.

He didn't say anything this time. He just watched.

But he felt closer. The veil that had once separated dream from waking reality had thinned.

Haylee jolted awake, her breath caught in her chest. She looked around the dim room, her eyes landing on Sam beside her. He was fast asleep, his arm loosely draped where she'd been resting.

She tucked herself gently under his arm, pressing her face into the curve of his shoulder. His arm tightened instinctively, pulling her in.

Safe. For now.

She closed her eyes again, hoping that the echoes of Elliot's presence would stay in the dream world.

But deep inside, she knew better.

Sunrise Stillness

Sam woke to an empty bed. His heart leapt into his throat.

"Haylee?" he called, already halfway out of the bedroom, his pulse quickening with every step. Visions of black feathers and strangers in shadows clouded his mind.

He found her on the porch, wrapped in a thick blanket, a steaming cup of tea cradled in her hands. The sky was still painted in pre-dawn hues, and the ocean breeze rolled in soft and cold.

She turned her head at the sound of his footsteps, offering him a small, tired smile.

"Hey," she said softly.

Sam didn't answer right away. He walked to her, knelt beside the chair, and wrapped his arms around her. She didn't resist—just leaned into him with a deep exhale.

"I didn't mean to worry you," she said after a moment.

"You didn't. Not really," he replied, though the relief in his voice betrayed him. "I just... after everything—"

"I know." She touched his cheek. "I couldn't sleep."

He didn't ask for details. He just held her.

They stayed that way as the sky began to lighten, casting soft gold over the waves. A quiet moment in a world that had given them so few lately.

"Thank you," she whispered.

"For what?"

"For being here. For always finding me."

He smiled and kissed the top of her head.

"Always."

The sun crested the horizon, and with it came the promise of another day—one they would face together.

Dust in the Distance

David had just stepped out onto his porch with a mug of lukewarm coffee when the sound of tires crunching gravel reached him. Riles was back from an early-morning supply run, but something was off.

The Jeep door didn't slam shut like usual. No casual whistle. No sarcastic greeting.

Riles walked up the steps stiffly, his eyes scanning the horizon behind him. David frowned. "You expecting someone?"

"Not anymore," Riles muttered, brushing past him and setting a small brown bag on the table. "We've got a problem."

David's gut tightened. "Tell me."

Riles pulled a folded sheet of paper from his jacket pocket and slid it across the table. A printed still frame—grainy but clear enough. A man, mid-thirties, standing just outside a government archive building in Salem.

"That's one of Ray's contacts," Riles said. "Or... was. He was supposed to deliver a packet of classified notes. Never showed."

David narrowed his eyes. "Is he missing?"

Riles nodded grimly. "Ray said the guy's apartment was cleared out. Like he vanished. No sign of a struggle, no signs of life."

David looked up. "This isn't just about Elliot anymore, is it?"

"No," Riles said, voice low. "There's an entire network being scrubbed. Quietly. Like someone's closing doors before we get through them."

They both fell silent, the weight of that realization sinking in. Then David spoke.

"We can't stay here. Not if we're being watched."

Riles raised an eyebrow. "You think they've found us?"

"I think it's only a matter of time."

A beat passed. Then David added, "We head out tonight. Call Haylee and Sam —have them meet us somewhere neutral."

Riles didn't argue.

They both looked out over the quiet Oregon landscape—morning light glinting off dew-covered trees. It looked peaceful.

But peace, they knew, was never more than a temporary illusion.

Desert Bound

The text came in just after breakfast.

David: Change of plans. We need to meet. Things are moving faster than we thought. Arizona. We'll send coordinates once we get settled.

Haylee sat on the edge of the porch, rereading the message three times before passing her phone to Sam.

He read it silently, then looked out at the ocean. "Well, I guess that's our cue."

They packed quietly. Kate and Meg noticed the shift in their energy—an urgency that hadn't been there the day before. Hugs were exchanged, promises made to keep in touch, and Lydia gave Josie a sloppy goodbye pat on the head. Bella, still aloof, blinked slowly from the passenger seat like a queen returning to her chariot.

The road south stretched wide and empty, winding them through evergreen forests, past snowy hillsides, and eventually into the sun-drenched openness of the Arizona desert.

By the second day, Haylee was feeling restless again. Being still had been comforting—but being in motion was necessary. Even Josie seemed to perk up as the warmth returned to the air, her ears flicking excitedly at the scent of distant desert critters.

Just after sunset, they found a small campground outside Sedona. Remote, quiet, tucked against a backdrop of red rocks that glowed ember-like in the fading light.

Sam guided Bertha into a narrow spot between two mesquite trees.

Haylee exhaled. "This will do."

They stepped out into the dusky air, stretching their legs, letting the quiet soak in.

Tomorrow, David and Riles would arrive.

Tonight, they'd rest and ready themselves for what was coming.

Letters left behind

The morning unfolded slowly—quiet and easy, as if the world itself was offering them a breath. Haylee moved through Bertha with practiced ease, prepping coffee while Sam took Josie for a short walk down the dusty campground trail. Bella lounged in a patch of sun near the back window, her tail flicking contentedly.

Haylee reached for the milk in the small fridge, but the cap slipped through her fingers and rolled under the couch with a soft clink.

With a sigh, she knelt down and reached underneath.

Fingertips brushing against cool metal, then something papery.

She pulled out the milk cap… and along with it, an envelope.

It was old—yellowed slightly with time, the edges soft and worn. On the front, in Aggie's handwriting:

Haylee — For when the road circles back.

Her heart skipped a beat.

She stared at it for a long moment before placing it on the counter and finishing the coffee. When Sam returned, cheeks pink from the crisp desert morning, she was already outside at the picnic table with two mugs and the envelope between them.

"What's this?" he asked, sitting down beside her.

"I found this under the couch, don't ask how," she said. "It's from Aggie."

Sam's eyes widened as he took a sip of the coffee she handed him. "She really did hide things in every corner of this RV."

Haylee nodded and turned the envelope over. There was a faint wax seal—cracked now, but bearing the familiar key sigil.

With steady fingers, she opened it.

Inside was a short letter and a faded photo of Aggie standing next to Bertha, her hand resting on the side mirror. But behind her, in the reflection of the glass—

Elliot.

It was subtle, almost unnoticeable, but he was there. Watching.

Haylee read aloud the letter, Aggie's voice echoing in her mind:

"If you found this, it means the road has brought you back to where the veil thins. Elliot's reach is longer than we thought, and his followers are no longer hiding. There is more in Bertha than I ever told you. Trust your instincts. Trust those who love you. The answers are layered. You'll have to be patient to see them clearly."

Sam's hand found hers across the table.

"Looks like Bertha still has more to say," he murmured.

Haylee nodded slowly, her eyes never leaving the photo.

"Yes… and we'd better be ready to listen."

Chapter Twenty-Six:
Shadows at Our Backs

The low rumble of tires crunching over gravel stirred Haylee from her thoughts. She stepped out of Bertha with a fresh pot of coffee in one hand and four mugs stacked in the other, just as Sam emerged behind her, stretching.

A familiar Jeep rolled up, dust trailing behind like a tail of tension.

David and Riles climbed out slowly. They looked worse for wear—unkempt, exhausted, eyes sharp from lack of sleep.

"You two look like hell," Sam said with a crooked smile as he approached.

"You should see the other guy," Riles muttered, rubbing the back of his neck.

"Rough night?" Haylee asked, already pouring the coffee into the mugs she'd set on the picnic table.

David nodded and accepted the steaming mug she handed him. "We couldn't shake the feeling we were being followed. Every time we checked the rearview, headlights were there. Then gone."

"Same car?" Sam asked, glancing at Riles.

Riles took a long sip before answering. "Not sure. Could've been. Could've been paranoia. But I trust my gut. And it wasn't nothing."

Haylee sat across from them, her own cup warming her hands. "It's not just paranoia. We've had things happen too.

Haylee looked down at the table, then over to Bertha. "We might already have one. Aggie left another letter. I found it this morning."

Four pairs of eyes locked, the tension thickening in the air.

"Well," Riles said, straightening up. "Let's hear it."

Haylee nodded. "After breakfast. We're going to need full stomachs for this."

Sam passed out plates of toast and eggs, sliding them across the table like a well-practiced diner cook.

"Breakfast is served," he said, offering a half-smile that didn't quite reach his eyes.

Riles snorted. "Luxury dining with a side of dread. Just how I like it."

They all managed a chuckle, the tension breaking slightly under the weight of warm food and familiar ritual.

Josie padded over from under the RV and settled beside Haylee, resting her head on Haylee's boot. Bella appeared next, leaping effortlessly onto the picnic table and curling up like a furry sentry.

David picked up his fork but didn't eat right away. "What exactly did Aggie say?"

Haylee didn't answer right away. Her fingers traced the rim of her coffee mug. "I'll let you read it for yourselves."

Riles shot a short grin, "Suspense, I like it."

The silence returned, this time thoughtful.

Trust in Strange Places

Riles leaned back, arms crossed, expression skeptical. "Bertha, your RV has been giving you clues?" he said with a half-believing smirk. "So what now?"

Haylee exchanged a glance with Sam, then looked back at Riles. "Just when we need it most, Bertha—or maybe Aggie—sends a message. Whether it's in a dream or something just shows up. I can't explain it any other way. I don't understand it myself, but I trust that Aggie is leading us to help."

David nodded slowly, the lines in his face deepening with thought. "Then maybe it's time we trust the message and prepare for what's coming. Together." Sam leaned forward, resting his elbows on the table. "We should travel together from now on. Safety in numbers."

"You two in the Jeep," Haylee added, "and we'll drive Bertha. There's plenty of room if you don't mind sharing the pull-out couch. It's not much, but at least it's warm. And safe—for now."

Riles laughed lightly. "I've slept on worse."

David grinned. "No problems here."

The group chuckled again, the tension melting just a bit more.

Haylee looked toward the horizon. "Then it's settled. We stay together. No more splitting up."

Sam reached for her hand beneath the table. "From here on out, we face everything—together."

As the day wore on, the group began to relax, lulled by the gentle rhythm of the desert around them. The stillness, broken only by the occasional birdcall or the whisper of wind through brush, provided a strange comfort.

They spent the afternoon together outside, playing card games on the picnic table and telling stories. Laughter came easier with each hand dealt, as though they were all shedding a layer of fear they didn't realize they were carrying.

Riles proved to be a terrible card player, bluffing with a wild grin that gave everything away. David, surprisingly sharp and competitive, took the game seriously and teased Riles mercilessly every time he lost.

Bella lounged on the RV's roof, flicking her tail, while Josie trotted between laps, begging for scraps and belly rubs.

Haylee leaned into Sam's shoulder at one point, a soft sigh escaping her lips. "I missed this. Just… people. Just breathing."

"Yeah," Sam said, brushing a kiss against her temple. "It feels good to laugh again."

As night fell, they lit a small fire in the pit near the campsite. The flames crackled, casting long shadows and warm light across their faces. They passed around mugs of cocoa and let the quiet settle again, this time with a kind of ease.

For the first time in what felt like ages, they weren't running.

Driftwood Days

The following morning brought with it a sky of soft blue and streaks of dusty gold. The air was cooler than the day before, and the wind carried a hint of something unspoken.

To stay productive, the group found ways to keep busy.

Haylee and David took Bertha into the nearest desert town for supplies— water, fuel, groceries, and anything they might need if they had to pack up quickly. The streets were quiet, lined with weather-worn shops and sun-bleached signs. Haylee showed David a small corner store where she and Sam had picked up some extra blankets. It felt strangely domestic—comfortable even—like a pocket of normalcy tucked between layers of chaos.

"I forgot what normal felt like," David said, examining a can of beans.

Haylee smirked. "This is our version of normal now."

Back at the campground, Sam and Riles took a more tactical approach. They walked the perimeter, making note of entry points and potential blind spots. They flagged the narrow gravel road as both a blessing and a curse—good for spotting anyone coming, bad if they needed to escape fast. Noting where shadows lingered longest and where their cell signal dropped. It was strategic but not obsessive—more about feeling prepared than being afraid.

"Feels too quiet," Riles muttered, crouching beside a cactus as he scanned the open expanse. "Like something's holding its breath."

Sam nodded. "Yeah. Haylee says the stillness doesn't feel peaceful anymore. Just paused."

They returned to camp as the sun slipped behind the mountains, casting the desert in amber hues. The night fell as it had the last few: quiet, uneventful, almost kind.

But it was the "almost" that lingered.

Evenings were filled with card games and long walks beneath the stars. Riles continued to lose spectacularly at cards, much to everyone's delight, and David had discovered an unexpected love for stargazing, pointing out constellations with a battered field guide he'd found tucked in the Jeep.

Bertha, too, began to feel like a fortress again. A safe place. At night, Sam and Haylee stole moments for themselves—quiet kisses shared under blankets, whispered hopes and fears, hands held tightly in the dark.

It was peaceful. Maybe not the kind that lasts, but the kind that gives strength. For now, that was enough.

The next few weeks passed in a slow, sun-warmed haze. Mornings began with the smell of fresh coffee drifting from Bertha's kitchenette and the sound of Bella hopping down from her perch to find the first patch of sunlight. Josie would nose her way out the door, ready for her walk, while Sam or David stretched with sleepy groans and Riles filled a small notebook with quiet observations.

There were no black feathers. No anonymous messages. No shadows slinking between trees. Just stillness.

For the first time in what felt like ages, no one was looking over their shoulder.

Haylee had returned to her journaling, finally able to hear her own thoughts without interruption. On the evening of February 3rd, she sat at the small table inside Bertha, legs tucked beneath her, pen moving in slow, thoughtful strokes across the page.

February 3rd, 2025

It's been quiet.

Too quiet, maybe—but I'm not complaining. Not really.

I didn't realize how much tension I'd been holding in my body until I finally let it go. Here, with all of them, there's been laughter again. Real, soul-deep laughter. And it's healing things I didn't know were broken.

David and I have started talking in a new way—like equals, not just father and daughter with history between us. Sam makes everything feel light even when it isn't. Bella's attitude has been impeccable (for her), and Josie snores like a cartoon character, which makes everyone smile.

But even in all this peace… something inside me is stirring. Like the road is calling again.

I keep thinking about Aggie's letter. About what it meant when she said "where the veil thins." I don't know where that is yet, but I get the feeling we're not meant to stay here too long. I wish I could explain it better than just a feeling, but that's all I have.

The stillness is beautiful—but movement has always been my compass. We'll leave soon. I don't know exactly where we're going, but I trust that when we need to know, we will.

Westward and Wary

The next morning, as if the journal entry had manifested its own momentum. Haylee felt it first, that itch beneath the surface of peace. She began rearranging cabinets in Bertha, checking the tires, and cleaning out the fridge. They'd be leaving soon.

Riles agreed without much persuasion. "If we're going to keep one step ahead, we can't get comfortable," he said, folding up his maps.

The decision came easily. It wasn't dramatic or urgent—just right. A stretch of new scenery, ocean breeze, winding roads and open sky. The kind of drive that could clear anyone's head.

David, having finally perfected his coffee routine with Bertha's finicky stove, didn't argue when Sam floated the idea: Let's head for the coast.

They took two days to prepare. Sam and Riles replaced the inverter, working shoulder to shoulder in the dust with grease-stained hands and matching grins. Haylee and David drove into town for fuel, bottled water, and a few replacement fuses. Bella supervised from the RV roof, tail twitching like a metronome. Josie napped in the sun, blissfully unaware of the urgency stirring beneath their calm.

The group began to pack up. Bertha hummed softly as her systems were checked, and David folded up maps with a sense of purpose.

The California coast was calling.

Sam stood beside Haylee as she closed her journal, sliding it into the glove compartment. He kissed her and gave her hand a squeeze.

"You ready?"

Haylee smiled, eyes reflecting the pale morning light. "More than ever."

When the day came, Bertha rumbled to life with a familiar shudder, and the Jeep took its place in the rearview.

They didn't rush. One night they pulled into a quiet rest area to let Josie stretch her legs, and share a meal of sandwiches. Another time, they stayed in a small RV park, blending in with other travelers—just faces on the road with stories no one asked about.

Each mile closer to the California coast brought fresh breath. Salt in the air. Movement beneath their wheels. It felt like freedom, even with shadows at their backs.

Bertha rolled on steadily—toward whatever was waiting.

Chapter Twenty-Seven:
Hearts in the Sand

They made their way slowly down the California coast, Bertha humming along the winding roads with the Jeep trailing close behind. It was early morning when they finally arrived at the campground near the beach, the salty air wrapping around them like a warm welcome.

The sound of waves crashing and gulls calling was a balm to the group, especially Riles, who had never set foot on a California beach before. His wide-eyed wonder as he stepped onto the boardwalk was enough to draw a laugh from David, who clapped him on the back.

"Told you," David said with a grin. "There's nothing like the coast."

The group took their time walking along the shore, dipping toes into the chilly water, exploring kitschy shops, and breathing in the fresh sea air. The tension of the past few weeks seemed to melt away with each crashing wave.

After a morning spent wandering, Haylee and Sam slipped away under the guise of a grocery run. David and Riles didn't question it—they saw the way the two kept stealing glances, craving a little space of their own.

In town, Sam ducked into a small boutique while Haylee picked out a bottle of wine and a charcuterie board. He returned with a small paper bag and a mischievous grin.

That evening, just before sunset, Sam led Haylee down a secluded stretch of beach. The sky was streaked in warm golds and pinks, and the cool sand softened underfoot.

Waiting for them was a cozy setup: a blanket spread out beside a carefully built bonfire, soft pillows, and flickering battery-operated lanterns casting a romantic glow. Scattered across the blanket were rose petals—faux, but still lovely in the dusky light.

Haylee gasped softly. "Sam... what is this?"

"Valentine's Day," he said simply. "I wanted tonight to feel like it's just us."

She set down the wine and snacks, and they sank into the blankets together, sharing food, stories, and quiet laughter as the sky darkened. The ocean whispered its lullaby beside them.

Later, they lay tangled in each other's arms, the fire crackling low beside them, the stars stretching endlessly overhead.

For one night, it was just the two of them—and everything else melted away.

Shoreline Mornings

The next morning arrived with a soft breeze and the rhythmic hush of the ocean waves. David was the first one up, rummaging quietly through Bertha's small kitchen, soon joined by Riles, who yawned and blinked against the light. "Coffee?" David offered.

"Only if it's strong enough to stand a spoon in it," Riles mumbled, rubbing the back of his neck.

As the pot brewed, the two men moved outside, steaming mugs in hand. The beach stretched before them, a canvas of golden sand and slow-moving waves. They spotted two figures nestled together down by the shoreline, partially buried in a drift of blankets and rose petals.

"The lovebirds made a nest," Riles said with a smirk.

"Let 'em sleep a little longer," David replied. "They earned it."

But just as he said it, Josie came tearing around the corner of Bertha, tail wagging, ears flapping in the breeze. She sprinted down the beach in a joyous blur, kicking up sand in all directions.

Haylee stirred first, brushing grains of sand from her cheek and sitting up slowly. She turned toward the sound of approaching paws.

"Is that—?"

"Incoming," Sam muttered just as Josie collided into them with a happy bark.

They both laughed, rising to their feet, brushing off sand as Josie circled them excitedly.

David and Riles walked up a moment later, each lifting a hand in sheepish greeting.

"Sorry," Riles said, trying not to laugh. "She got away from us."

"At least she didn't bring the coffee with her," David added, raising his mug.

Haylee grinned, her cheeks flushed from the morning chill and laughter. She turned to Sam and gave him a warm smile, the kind that made everything feel right again.

Bella, ever the diva, stretched languidly in the open doorway of Bertha, then leapt gracefully to the dash where she perched like royalty, gazing out at the beach with mild disdain.

"That cat has more attitude than all of us combined," Riles muttered.

"And she knows it," Sam said.

The morning passed with ease and laughter. After a quick breakfast, the group decided to explore the nearby cliffs and tide pools. With no signs of danger, no black feathers, and no cryptic letters—just sunshine and sea breeze—it felt, if only for a while, like a new beginning.

They packed lightly, took Bertha up the coastal road a bit, and parked near a scenic overlook. Cameras were pulled out, jokes flew freely, and even David cracked a rare smile when Riles slipped on a patch of seaweed.

As the afternoon sun glinted across the waves, Haylee looked around at the people she loved—her found family—and for the first time in weeks, she didn't feel like she was running.

She felt like she had arrived.

Chapter Twenty-Eight:
Salt and Shadows

They found seashells scattered like treasures along the shore, each discovery followed by laughter and playful teasing. Josie splashed in the shallow surf with Haylee and Sam, barking joyfully as waves rolled over her paws. Bella trailed behind cautiously, her paws daintily avoiding the water, but she stayed close.

David and Riles, ever the silent sentinels, kept a loose watch over the area, their eyes scanning the horizon, but even they let down their guard enough to enjoy the day. The weight of responsibility lifted, if only slightly.

The group's wandering led them to a small event near the boardwalk—an impromptu festival complete with a balloon artist twisting colorful creations, children getting their faces painted, and families gathered around arts and crafts tables. The smell of cotton candy and grilled hot dogs mingled in the air.

Haylee found a quaint shell necklace at one of the vendor stalls, the pendant delicate and glinting like sea glass. Sam grinned and gave Josie a bite of his turkey sandwich while Haylee captured the afternoon on video for her YouTube channel—something she realized she had been neglecting.

"You're getting back into it," Sam said, watching her film. "Feels like a good day for a comeback."

"Yeah," she nodded, smiling. "It does."

David and Riles leaned against the railing nearby, sipping iced coffees and observing the crowd. "Simple days like this," David said, "are worth everything."

Just as Sam and Haylee posed for a selfie on the boardwalk, their smiles wide and carefree, Haylee's phone buzzed.

He glanced at the notification. Then his expression changed.

Haylee leaned in to look.

A text from an Unknown number:

"You think you're being clever."

Their stomachs dropped in unison.

Sam's arm lowered slowly, the phone still in hand.

"David," he called, his voice tight. "Riles."

The men were at their side in seconds.

No one said a word at first. The message said enough. The day's calm fractured under a single sentence.

They all scanned the crowd—but whoever had sent it was already gone.

The joy of the day lingered only a second longer before vanishing into the breeze.

The rest of the day continued in quiet unease. After the text, the group returned to the campground, keeping an eye over their shoulders, speaking in low tones. The shadow of whoever had followed them hung thick in the air. Even Josie was subdued, curling up close to Haylee's feet beneath the picnic table as if she sensed the mood.

That evening, they sat around the campfire. The flames cracked and snapped, sending sparks spiraling into the darkening sky. Sam stared into the fire, silent, while Haylee thumbed her phone over and over again, rereading the message. David stood a few feet away, arms crossed, scanning the perimeter of the campground as if daring the sender to show themselves.

"They're watching us," Riles finally said. "Not just following—we're under surveillance."

Haylee swallowed hard. "We should move again."

David shook his head. "No. Not yet. They want us unsettled. If we keep running, we'll never find their weakness."

Riles nodded. "We stay put. Fortify. Watch who watches us."

Sam reached over and took Haylee's hand, grounding her. "And if they come closer?"

David's voice was firm. "Then we remind them they're not the only ones watching."

The following morning dawned gray and cool. Fog drifted in from the sea, ghosting through the campground. Haylee sat with a mug of coffee in hand, bundled in Sam's hoodie, staring at the horizon.

Bella perched beside her on the picnic table, tail flicking with more agitation than usual.

Sam came up behind her, wrapping his arms around her shoulders. "You okay?"

Haylee nodded slowly. "Just waiting for the other shoe to drop."

He rested his chin on her shoulder. "Let's make them wait instead."

She managed a soft smile.

Behind them, David and Riles were already packing up some gear—just in case. The calm of the beach, once so soothing, now felt like a trap.

But they weren't done fighting. Not yet.

They just had to be ready.

The Bait We Cast

Two days passed with no messages, no feathers, no shadowy figures in the crowd. Just silence.

Too much silence.

Riles didn't like it.

"They're watching," he said one morning, pacing near the fire pit. "They're waiting for us to slip up."

David sipped his coffee, eyes narrowed toward the tree line. "So let's give them what they want."

Haylee looked up from her journal. "What do you mean?"

"We make them think you're alone," Riles said. "Stage it. You stay at the RV, we take the Jeep. Act like we've split up. You'll be bait."

Sam's jaw clenched. "Absolutely not."

Haylee reached for his hand. "Sam… maybe he's right."

Riles held up both hands. "We'll stay close. You won't be alone for real. David and I will circle back and hide near the RV. Sam, you can choose—go with us or stay close but out of sight."

Sam's gaze dropped to the ground, conflicted.

"If they come," Riles added, "we grab one. Talk to them. See what they know." "And if they don't talk?" Sam asked.

Riles looked at David. Their silence said enough.

"No torture," Haylee said flatly. "We do this my way."

David nodded reluctantly. "We can work with that."

They put the plan into action the next morning. Sam kissed Haylee goodbye a little too long for show, then "reluctantly" got into the Jeep with David and Riles. The RV door closed behind her as Bertha sat quiet and seemingly unguarded beneath a pale, overcast sky.

Haylee waited.

A few hours later, the watcher appeared.

He was younger than she expected—early twenties maybe. Lean, jittery. Not a professional. He circled the RV, glancing over his shoulder too often.

The moment he stepped toward Bertha, David and Riles moved in from behind the trees. Sam stepped out from the shadows beside the rig.

"Going somewhere?" Riles growled, shoving the kid against the side of the RV.

They dragged him to a folding chair behind the fire ring, zip-tied his hands, and began asking questions.

He didn't talk right away. He fidgeted. Spit. Cursed.

But Haylee sat across from him, calm. Patient. Eventually, he broke.

Said he didn't know Elliot personally—only that a group had been following her for weeks. He claimed to be a runner. Said something about "The Return" and a place called *The Fold*.

When pressed for names or locations, he clammed up.

After hours, Haylee stood and said, "Let him go."

David balked. "He could lead us to more."

"Or he could be bait himself," Haylee said. "Letting him go sends the message: We're not afraid of them."

They left him with water, untied his wrists, and sent him walking.

Only once he was out of sight did anyone speak.

"You trust what he said?" Riles asked.

Haylee shook her head. "No. But it was still something."

Silent Truths

Later that evening, while the others prepped dinner, Sam found Haylee sitting alone on a driftwood log near the edge of the campground. Josie sat at her feet, chewing on a stick, while Bella prowled a few feet away, chasing a fluttering moth with uncharacteristic energy.

Sam settled beside her, nudging her knee gently. "Hey."

"Hey," she replied, eyes still fixed on the horizon.

"You've been quiet."

Haylee took a deep breath. "I keep thinking about that guy we let go. What if he lied? What if we just showed them that we're merciful—and weak?"

"You're not weak," Sam said, his voice low. "You made a call based on hope, not fear. That takes strength."

She looked at him, searching his face for something solid. "I just... I hate the not knowing. I hate feeling like bait."

Sam reached into his pocket and pulled out a smooth stone, warm from the fire. He placed it in her hand. "Then take this. Every time you feel like the world's out to get you, remember you're grounded. You're not alone."

Haylee smiled faintly, curling her fingers around the stone.

Meanwhile, back at the picnic table, David and Riles cleaned up dishes in near silence.

"She's tougher than she looks," Riles said, finally breaking the quiet.

David gave a grunt of agreement. "She's got more of Aggie in her than she realizes."

Riles dried a plate with a faded dish towel. "Still think we should've leaned on that guy a little harder?"

David shook his head. "No. She needed to do it her way. We've seen too much of the other side of that."

Josie trotted over, tail wagging, a crumpled paper plate in her mouth. She deposited it proudly at Riles' feet.

Riles chuckled. "Thanks, sanitation crew."

Bella followed shortly after, leaping gracefully onto the table and flicking her tail like she had supervised the entire cleanup.

David smirked. "If we're ever in a real mess, maybe we just let the animals take over."

Riles nodded, deadpan. "Might be the smartest ones in the group."

They laughed—an easy, genuine sound that wrapped around the firelight like a promise.

For now, they were safe.

But not for long.

Anchor in the Fog

Haylee didn't sleep much that night, her thoughts a restless tide. But every time she stirred, jolting from half-dreams and half-dread, Sam was there. A steady presence.

She curled into his chest just before dawn, head tucked beneath his chin. His breathing deep and even, until her fingers lightly brushed his arm. He woke gently, turning to find her wide-eyed, watching him.

Without a word, he pressed a kiss to her forehead and wrapped his arms tighter around her. She exhaled, letting the warmth of him melt the last of her fear.

Their love, quiet and unshakable, felt like armor against the chaos closing in. Later that morning, Haylee sat by the RV's open door, sunlight catching the edges of her coffee mug. A string of notifications lit up her phone— comments and reactions to the beach footage she'd finally posted to her long-neglected YouTube channel.

The praise came flooding in:

"Your video made me feel like I was there."

"That ocean sunset—pure magic."

"Josie and the waves had me smiling all day."

For a moment, she was back in the real world—the one filled with cozy strangers, kind words, and ordinary beauty. The contrast was jarring, but grounding.

She smiled to herself and opened her journal.

February 26, 2025

This morning feels still. Peaceful. I'm trying to hold onto it for as long as I can. Sam is still asleep—he's become my lighthouse, steady and warm, always pointing me home even when the fog rolls in thick. He's everything I never knew I needed.

David and Riles... I'm beginning to understand them more. I know why they're protective. Why they're sharp-edged when I need softness. They care in their own way.

I don't regret letting that scout go. He wasn't a threat. He was a message. I don't know what it said exactly, but I think it's clearer now: We're not meant to fight fire with fire. We're meant to outsmart it. Outlast it.

We'll keep watching. We'll stay alert. But we won't stop living.

Not now. Not ever.

Between Frequencies

Two days passed in an uneasy calm.

No new texts. No new sightings. But no one relaxed,—not really.

Then, early one morning, David's phone lit up with an encrypted ping—Ray.

He stepped away from the RV, thumbing the call to life with a quiet urgency.

"Ray?"

A breath, and then Ray's voice—rough, tired, but unmistakably his. "Where are you?"

"We're in California."

David scanned the sleepy campground. "Not sure for how long."

"We had contact?" David said sharply.

"What, how, when?" Ray asked with a lump in his throat.

David hesitated. "One of Elliot's scouts tried to make a move a couple of days ago. We intercepted him. Got some info—but it's foggy."

Ray let out a string of low curses. "Stupid move, if he wasn't sanctioned."

"You think he went rogue?" David asked.

"Either that," Ray said, "or it was a test. See how close they could get without setting off alarms. But if they're breaking protocol, that means Elliot's reach is spreading... and getting sloppy. Or desperate."

David's jaw tightened. "So we're not just being watched. We're being measured."

There was silence on the line before Ray continued, more sober now. "Just be careful. Don't assume the next one is there to talk. I've been underground for a reason—too many people sniffing around. But I'll send you something. New intel later."

"Okay," David said. "And Ray—stay safe. We can't afford to lose you."

"I'm not going anywhere," Ray replied. "Not until she's safe."

The line went dead.

David stood still for a moment, watching the early light pour over the dunes.

The silence pressed in around him.

But it wasn't empty.

It was waiting.

Chapter Twenty-Nine:
Guardians Unveiled

The morning sun filtered through the thin curtains in Bertha, casting golden stripes across Haylee's journal. She sat at the fold-out table, pen in hand, chewing gently on the cap.

Sam, David, and Riles were still stretching off the night before, each of them sluggish but alert. No one had really rested—not fully—not since Ray's call.

Haylee looked up as Sam stepped inside, rubbing the sleep from his eyes. "You ready?" she asked.

"Yeah," he said with a yawn. "David's making coffee. Riles is already checking the Jeep."

They all met at the picnic table a few minutes later, mugs in hand.

David got straight to it. "We need to talk about what Ray said."

Haylee nodded. "Elliot's reach is growing. But something else is growing too. I think... Bertha knows."

Riles raised a brow. "Bertha? The RV?"

"She's more than that," Haylee said softly. "She's... connected somehow. Like a conduit. When I trust my gut, she responds. Yesterday morning, Bella led me to something."

Sam looked to the RV. "What did you find?"

Haylee stood and walked over to Bertha's side, opening a storage hatch. Inside, an etched panel pulsed faintly with a soft, otherworldly glow. She brushed her fingers across it, revealing a sigil—the same one Aggie used to seal her letters.

Bella, perched on the dashboard, gave a low trill and leapt down, sitting beside Haylee as if guarding the symbol.

"That's new," David said, leaning in. "It wasn't there yesterday."

"Exactly," Haylee said. "Bertha reveals things only when we're ready."

Bella meowed once, then walked in a circle around the glowing panel before settling beside it with a watchful gaze.

Through the Watcher's Eyes

That night, Haylee couldn't sleep. She sat cross-legged on the bed, Bella curled at her side.

The cat's eyes glowed faintly in the moonlight, and for a moment, Haylee swore she saw something shimmer in the air—like a mist between realities.

Her vision tunneled. The RV faded away. She was standing in the woods outside Aggie's old cabin. Moonlight pooled across the clearing. The air was heavy with memory.

Aggie's voice drifted in, gentle and warm.

"You're doing well, my girl. Don't doubt yourself now."

Haylee turned—and there Aggie stood, solid and smiling. Not a dream. Not a memory. A presence.

"Bella sees what others miss. Trust her. She's your link when the road goes dim."

Haylee opened her mouth to speak, but the air shifted again—and Aggie was gone.

The woods faded. Bertha returned.

Bella was staring at her with deep, knowing eyes.

Haylee whispered, "You're more than you seem, huh?"

Bella blinked slowly, then rested her head against Haylee's arm.

And outside, the wind whispered through the trees.

It was time to return to Aggie's cabin.

A New Path Forward

The next morning, Haylee didn't wait. After Sam brewed coffee, she gathered everyone at the picnic table and laid it all out.

"I had a vision," she said plainly.

David, mid-sip, stilled. Riles arched an eyebrow. Sam just sat quietly, letting her speak.

"It wasn't a dream. It felt different—real. I saw Aggie… and the cabin. She said Bella sees what others miss. That she's my link when the road goes dim."

David leaned forward. "You're saying Bella is some kind of… guide?"

Haylee shrugged. "I don't know. But Aggie said I'd be found by a guardian if she wasn't around. Bella showed up out of nowhere, at a campground. Just made herself a home in Bertha."

Riles rubbed his chin. "So, what—you think she was sent?"

"I think she chose me," Haylee said. "Or was sent to find me. Either way, she's more than just a cat."

Bella, as if on cue, strutted across the table and sat right in front of David, meeting his eyes like she dared him to argue.

He held her gaze a moment, then sighed. "Fair enough."

Then Riles asked, "So what now?"

"We go to the cabin," Haylee said. "That's where the next piece is."

Sam nodded. "We can leave by morning."

David added, "We'll need to be careful. If the cabin is as connected as Bertha, we might not be the only ones who feel it."

Riles stood and stretched. "Then let's pack light and get some rest. Sounds like the next road's going to be a strange one."

Bella flicked her tail and turned toward the RV, already heading inside like she knew the way.

Return to the Pines

The road twisted tighter the deeper they drove into the hills, the air growing colder, more still.

Haylee sat in the passenger seat of Bertha, fingers tracing the edge of the old map they'd once used to find the cabin. She hadn't unfolded it in a long time, but it guided them true—just like before.

The tires crackled over loose gravel and leaves as they pulled up to the same narrow clearing, barely wide enough to turn around. It looked exactly the same.

"It hasn't changed," Haylee whispered.

Bertha came to a gentle stop beside the tree line. The trees loomed tall and dense, their limbs heavy with silence.

David pulled in behind them in the Jeep. As everyone climbed out, a quiet fell over the group.

Haylee stepped forward, feeling the chill run up her spine just like it had the first time. The cabin hunched beneath a canopy of towering pines, weathered and stubborn. Moss still clung to the roof. The windows were still boarded. The front door still hung askew, creaking faintly in the wind.

Bella leapt from the RV before anyone else had moved. Her ears were perked, her tail raised high. She trotted ahead as if she knew exactly where she was going, and then she sat—poised and waiting—at the foot of the front steps.

Sam stepped up beside Haylee. "Déjà vu?"

"Exactly," she said.

Josie sniffed the air and followed Bella, then laid down beside the steps as if standing guard.

Riles circled the perimeter, his hand unconsciously resting on his belt, scanning the tree line.

David walked to the door and gave it a slight push. The hinges groaned, and the door eased inward.

"Still creepy," he muttered.

But Haylee didn't hesitate.

She stepped inside, the others following close behind.

The cabin was dustier than she remembered, but it still pulsed with a strange quiet. As if the air held memories in its lungs, waiting to exhale.

Bella padded across the wooden floor toward a small trunk near the fireplace —one Haylee hadn't noticed the first time. She sat beside it and meowed once.

Haylee glanced at Sam, then at David and Riles. None of them said a word.

She moved toward the trunk, heart thudding, and slowly lifted the lid.

Inside was a folded piece of paper sealed with a wax stamp—the same key sigil.

And beside it, a candle wrapped in worn velvet.

Haylee's hands trembled as she reached for the letter.

"Aggie." she whispered.

It read:

"If I'm not there, a guardian will find her. She won't be alone."
—Aggie

They were quiet for a long moment.

The Beacon Within

Everyone spread out through the cabin, searching quietly. Dust motes danced in the light filtering through the cracks in the boarded-up windows. The silence felt weighty—like the walls were holding their breath.

Riles stepped outside to check the perimeter, with Josie at his side, her ears perked and nose twitching. The dog seemed to be taking her role as protector seriously.

Inside, Haylee moved slowly, brushing her fingertips across the walls and shelves. She wasn't sure what she was looking for, but something inside her pulsed—like a soft tug from within.

Then, a sharp, focused ping pressed behind her eyes. Not pain. Just a sudden, intuitive pull.

She stopped. Turned.

Bella sat beside an old, slanted bookshelf. Her eyes were locked on Haylee. The ping returned—stronger this time.

Haylee stepped toward the shelf. Her skin tingled, as if electricity danced along her arms.

"Sam," she called softly. "Come here."

He appeared beside her, concern on his face. "What is it?"

"I think... I can feel something. It's like my body knows where to look."

Sam looked to Bella. "She led you here?"

Haylee nodded, crouching beside the shelf. She pulled it away from the wall and spotted a loose floorboard beneath.

"Got something," she whispered.

As Sam helped lift the board, Haylee reached in and retrieved a small wooden box, wrapped in faded cloth. The moment her fingers touched it, the tingling sensation intensified.

She met Sam's eyes. "It's happening again."

Sam gave her a steady look. "Then let's see what your instincts have to show us."

Signals in the Soil

While the others stayed inside, Riles made his way around the back of the cabin with Josie close behind. The dog sniffed with purpose, her body alert, every so often letting out a low growl.

Riles crouched near the edge of the property line where the brush thickened and spotted something half-buried in the dirt—rusted metal teeth protruding from the ground. A trap.

His brows furrowed.

"What the hell…?" he muttered, clearing away more debris.

There were two more. Old, but still dangerous. Whoever had placed them wasn't aiming for wildlife. The pattern, the placement—it was strategic.

He whistled low, and Josie came to stand by his side, growling softly.

"Shit. This isn't just some forgotten shack," Riles said under his breath.

He jogged back around the front and pushed open the cabin door. "Guys," he called, "you'll want to see this."

David stepped outside first, followed by Sam and Haylee.

Riles motioned for them to follow him around to the back. When they reached the spot, he pointed at the uncovered traps.

David crouched low. "Booby traps?"

"Strategically placed," Riles said. "Like someone was expecting to be hunted. Or worse—was trying to keep something out."

Haylee shivered. "You think Aggie set these?"

"Either her or someone trying to protect her," Riles said. "Either way, this wasn't just a hiding spot. This place was prepared for something."

Bella, perched nearby on a fallen log, watched them all with alert, glowing eyes.

Haylee looked to Sam. "We're not alone out here. We never were."

He nodded solemnly. "No."

Beneath the Dust

Haylee walked back inside while the others processed the significance of the traps. Her fingers brushed over the edges of the box she had just uncovered, the faded cloth still wrapped loosely around it.

She hadn't yet opened it when Riles came back in, his boots heavy on the old wood floor. He paused when he saw the box in her hands.

"What's that?" he asked.

Haylee looked down at it. "I don't know. I just found it under the floorboard."

Riles gave her a cautious look, half-curious, half-wary. "Why were you looking under the floorboards?"

"I wasn't. I just... got this feeling when I was near it. And Bella was sitting by the spot."

Riles didn't laugh. He didn't scoff. But the line of his mouth tightened. He didn't dismiss her, but he didn't fully understand, either.

Haylee slowly opened the box.

Inside, nestled in dark velvet, was a single skeleton key. Old, heavy, and tarnished.

"A key?" Sam asked, stepping forward.

"But to what?" David added, looking around the cabin.

The group fanned out again, checking every locked drawer, cabinet, and old chest in sight—but nothing fit the key.

Just as Haylee was starting to think it was symbolic more than literal, Bella let out a sharp meow. Everyone turned.

The cat was sitting next to a wall near the fireplace, tail curled neatly around her paws. Watching.

"Bella?" Haylee said softly.

She stepped toward her, and as she did, the ping returned—bright and sure behind her eyes.

"I'm getting it again," she said, her voice low.

She pressed her hand to the wall—and noticed something strange. Behind the layers of dust, there was a faint shimmer. A shape.

She wiped it clean with her sleeve and gasped.

A keyhole.

"What the hell... this wasn't here before," she whispered.

Everyone gathered around, eyes wide. No one spoke.

With shaking fingers, Haylee pulled the skeleton key from the box and placed it into the hidden lock.

It slid in smoothly. A click echoed through the cabin as the wall shifted slightly, revealing the outline of a concealed door.

They all looked at one another, stunned.

Bella sat back and flicked her tail.

Haylee took a breath.

"Looks like Aggie left us more than memories."

Sam's hand found hers.

And with a glance at the others, Haylee turned the knob.

Chapter Thirty:
A Place That Remembers

Behind the hidden door was a large room—much bigger than the outer cabin would suggest. From the outside, there had been no indication this space existed. It had been cloaked, concealed by something more than clever carpentry. Magic.

Haylee started to step forward, but Sam placed a gentle hand on her arm.

"We don't know what's in there," he said, his voice low.

Bella, unbothered, darted into the room.

"Bella!" Haylee called after her.

Sam turned on his phone flashlight, casting a beam across the threshold. Then, hand in hand, he and Haylee stepped inside. David and Riles followed, the latter resting his palm on the grip of his gun, eyes scanning.

The room felt like a sanctuary—and a vault. Bookshelves stretched from floor to ceiling, filled with leather-bound journals, herb jars, candles in every size, and rows of aged tomes with spines etched in faded gold. A faint, herbal scent hung in the air—lavender, sage, and something older.

On the inside of the door they'd just entered was a glowing sigil. It pulsed faintly, like a heartbeat.

Riles took position near the door, Josie settling beside him. Guarding.

Haylee drifted forward slowly, letting go of Sam's hand. The air shimmered faintly around her. Then—

A vision.

Aggie stood at the far end of the room, not as a memory, but vibrant and present, as if she'd only just stepped into the light.

"Haylee," she said gently, "there is much for you to learn. This is where you start."

And then she was gone.

Haylee stood frozen for a moment, her breath caught.

"Haylee?" Sam asked, stepping closer. "Are you okay?"

She nodded, though her eyes were distant. "I saw Aggie again. She said this is where I need to start."

No one spoke. The weight of the moment wrapped around them like fog.

They had crossed a threshold—not just into a room, but into something far greater.

Truths Held

The fire crackled faintly in the hearth, casting flickers of light across the room lined with secrets. They'd cleared a space on the floor with old rugs and cushions, settling into a circle like gravity had pulled them into place.

Haylee leaned against Sam, his warmth a quiet reassurance. Bella curled on a nearby windowsill, her eyes half-closed but alert.

David sat against a low bookshelf, elbows on his knees, eyes fixed on the sigil still glowing on the door.

Haylee sipped her tea—lavender and something ancient—and waited.

"So," she said gently, "how much did you know?"

David didn't look at her right away. He exhaled slowly, like he'd been holding this breath for years.

"I knew more than I told you," he admitted. "About Aggie. About what she was capable of."

Haylee's eyes narrowed—not in anger, but in quiet realization.

Sam shifted a little but stayed silent.

Riles raised an eyebrow. "Define 'capable.'"

David rubbed his hands together. "She had... access. Knowledge. Things passed down through our family, but hidden. Most didn't believe it anymore. But Aggie—she kept it alive. She didn't just believe. She practiced."

"And you?" Haylee asked.

"I watched. I listened. She tried to teach me once, when we were teenagers. Said we all had a spark, but it didn't wake up for everyone. I didn't want to know, not really. Thought it was too much. But I saw what she could do. Little things, at first. Then... bigger."

Haylee's voice was soft. "Why didn't you tell me?"

"Because I wanted you to have a normal life," he said. "Because part of me hoped you'd never have to see what she saw. But now—" he gestured around the hidden room, "there's no denying any of it. And you're already farther into this than she ever let me be."

Haylee nodded slowly. Bella jumped onto her lap and curled up like punctuation to the truth.

"I think she knew this would happen," Haylee said. "Maybe not all of it, but enough."

"Then this place," Sam added, "it's more than just a hideaway."

"It's a training ground," Riles muttered. "A vault. A sanctuary."

"Or a last resort," David added quietly.

They all looked around again. The books, the symbols, the quiet hum in the air. Haylee met David's gaze. "No more secrets.

He gave a small nod. "No more."

Later, after they'd explored the hidden room and unearthed the first few threads of its secrets, the group gathered around the old table just outside the cabin. The night was still, the air thick with pine and the promise of answers.

David hadn't spoken in some time. He stared into his coffee like it might reflect something he wasn't ready to face.

"Dad," Haylee said softly, "there's more, isn't there?"

He glanced up.

"When you were little," he began, "after the summers you spent with Aggie… you came back different. You had—abilities."

Haylee blinked. "What?"

"You scared us. Me. Your mother," David continued, his voice low with shame. "You'd say things before they happened. You'd talk about people's emotions like you could feel them. Once, you even stopped the lights from flickering just by touching the wall."

Haylee looked stunned. "Why didn't you tell me?"

"Because we told you it wasn't real," David admitted. "We said you were imagining things. We made you doubt yourself."

"But why?" she asked, scorn heavy in her tone.

David sighed, deeply. "Because I was afraid. I didn't want you to get hurt—or worse, have someone else see you doing those things. Kids can be cruel, Haylee. But their parents? Even worse. Judgmental. Fearful. You remember what happened later in the fall?"

Haylee's brows furrowed. Then her expression shifted.

"Yeah," she murmured. "I told my friends about what I'd done all summer instead of going to camp. About Aggie, and what she taught me. They laughed. Said I was making it up. My best friend's mom wouldn't even let me sleep over anymore."

David nodded. "Exactly. It broke your heart. And I—" he swallowed hard, "— I told Aggie to stop teaching you."

Haylee stared into the woods for a long beat, jaw clenched, tears prickling in her eyes. "You didn't protect me. You buried me."

"I know," he said, brokenly. "And I was wrong. I see that now."

No one spoke.

Then Riles shifted his weight and said, "Well. You're not normal. None of us are anymore. So... what now?"

Haylee looked up, fierce and resolute.

"Now we start over. With the truth."

Night Beneath the Pines

Everyone decided to call it a night. The day had revealed more than secret rooms and childhood fibs—it had peeled back layers of fear, of truth, of what it meant to be connected by blood, by legacy, and by choice.

They climbed into Bertha one by one, the RV creaking softly as if welcoming them back into its steel embrace. The forest outside whispered low through the trees, and the glow from the cabin faded behind the windows.

Haylee and Sam curled up in the bed, Bella settling at their feet like a sentinel in silk. Josie took her place by the door, her ears twitching every now and then, ever the guardian.

Despite the warmth, the air in Bertha felt different than in the cabin—charged, almost reverent. It wasn't fear, but something older, deeper. As if the RV recognized the change in its passengers.

No one said anything about it. But they all felt it.

If you looked back toward the cabin from a certain angle, it shimmered—not in the moonlight, but with something else entirely. An aura. A presence. Not just shade and structure, but something watching back.

Haylee lay awake a little longer, listening to the silence, tracing Bella's outline with her eyes in the dark.

Bertha had secrets. The cabin did too.

And Haylee? She was ready to uncover them all.

Tomorrow, they would deal with whatever came.

When the Silence Speaks

Haylee couldn't sleep.

She kept trying to remember the summers with Aggie. But the memories were faint, scattered like fireflies in a jar she could no longer open. Quietly, she slipped out of Bertha, careful not to wake Sam. Only Josie and Bella stirred— one alert and protective, the other gliding silently at her heels.

She crept back to the hidden room inside the cabin, its air cool and humming with something half-alive. Haylee sank to the floor, her back against a bookshelf. She opened one journal after another, flipping through faded pages inked with Aggie's looping handwriting. Bella hopped onto a shelf and curled up, while Josie stood sentry in the doorway.

The more she read, the more her questions multiplied. About Aggie. About herself. About who her real father was. Did he know about her? Was he like Aggie?

The journals spoke in riddles—half-poems, metaphors, veiled memories. Words danced just out of reach.

Somewhere between the lines and exhaustion, Haylee's eyes closed.

She dreamt.

She was a child again. The cabin looked almost the same, but warmer. Aggie was there, smiling, coaxing her gently. She showed her how to breathe through her palms, how to feel energy pulse through her skin.

Haylee laughed, awed by the invisible currents she could call with a thought. Then the dream shifted.

The hidden door stood ajar. Haylee wandered toward it. As she stepped inside, pain bloomed behind her eyes.

"It's too much, Aunt Aggie," she cried.

Aggie was suddenly there, pulling her back, closing the door with a firm hand. Haylee wept in her arms. "I'm sorry," she sobbed.

"No, child," Aggie whispered. "You did well. You're just not ready yet."

The dream dissolved like smoke.

Haylee slept on, the journal open in her lap, Bella watched over her with silent, golden eyes.

Chapter Thirty-One:
The Weight of Quiet Hours

Sam woke to an empty space beside him.

His hand reached out instinctively, brushing cold sheets where Haylee should've been. He sat up, tension blooming in his chest. Quietly slipping out of bed.

Bertha's steps creaked softly under Sam's bare feet as he stepped outside into the chill before dawn. A pale glow edged the horizon. The cabin loomed in a soft silhouette.

He pushed the door open and spotted a flicker of light from the hidden room.

He found Josie sitting alert at the door, tail wagging once as if to say, She's okay.

Inside, Haylee sat on the floor, her back against the shelves, journals and books spread around her like offerings. Bella perched on a shelf above her, tail curled neatly around her paws.

Sam stood at the threshold for a moment, watching her. Something about the way she looked in that moment—barefoot, half-asleep, determined—etched itself into him.

She stirred, feeling his gaze before she saw him.

"What time is it?" she asked, rubbing her eyes.

"Around 4 a.m.," Sam said, stepping in. "What are you doing out here? Alone?"

Haylee smiled faintly, glancing at her companions. "I'm not alone."

Before Sam could reply, Bella stretched toward a higher shelf. A book tumbled with a sharp *thud* onto the floor between them. Both jumped.

Sam crouched, reaching for it. It was heavier than expected, its leather cover cracked with age. A single symbol adorned the front—a key circled in ink, the same sigil they'd seen before.

But this one had no title. No name. Just the sigil, glowing faintly in the low light.

"What is it?" Haylee asked, now fully awake.

"I don't know," Sam murmured, turning it over in his hands. "But I think Bella wanted us to find it."

Bella leapt down from the shelf, brushed her head against Haylee's shoulder, then sat, eyes fixed on the book.

Sam helped Haylee up, and together they opened the cover.

It creaked like something ancient being disturbed—and within the first page was a sentence written in Aggie's unmistakable hand:

"Some doors open only in silence. Others require the courage to knock."

Haylee swallowed, the pulse behind her eyes beginning again—soft, familiar. A ping.

The air grew still around them.

The weight of the moment hung between their shared breaths.

Sam whispered, "I think we just knocked."

Before the Light Breaks

As Sam and Haylee turned through the worn pages of the sigil-marked book, a quiet energy crackled between them—like the room itself was listening.

Back in Bertha, David stirred. He blinked at the empty bedrolls, a low sense of unease tugging at him.

"Riles," he said, nudging the other man. "We're the only ones in here."

Riles sat up immediately, groggy but alert. "Where the hell did they go?"

The two men grabbed jackets and boots, stepping outside into the pine-dark stillness just before dawn. The door to the cabin was ajar. They moved quickly, tension building with every step.

Inside the hidden room, Haylee and Sam were hunched over the open book, heads nearly touching. Josie thumped her tail once when she saw David and Riles—greeting, not alarm.

David let out a breath. "What are you two up to?"

Riles squinted toward the window. "It's nearly dawn."

Haylee looked up and handed David the book. "Have you ever seen this before?"

He studied the sigil, running a thumb over the worn leather. "Looks familiar, but... I can't place it."

Sam helped Haylee to her feet, and the four of them made their way back to Bertha.

Haylee moved to the small kitchen, setting water to boil. The smell of brewing coffee slowly eased the tension. Outside, birds began their morning calls.

Sam clipped a leash on Josie and headed into the woods, choosing a different trail than the one they'd used to first approach the cabin. The morning air was sharp and damp. As they walked, Josie pulled suddenly toward a thicket, sniffing and circling.

That's when Sam saw it—an old animal trap, rusted and hidden by moss and bramble. Another, a few feet away, sprung long ago. It hadn't caught anything in years… but it hadn't been placed randomly either.

Sam crouched, brushing back the weeds. Someone had once taken great care to set these far from plain sight.

This wasn't a hunting trail. This had been a perimeter.

Josie whined softly.

"Let's go," he said quietly, eyes scanning the trees.

Back at Bertha, Sam relayed what he'd found. Riles' jaw tightened. "We need to sweep the area. Thoroughly."

"After breakfast," David said. "Then we gear up and get serious."

Just as Sam finished sharing what he'd found, Bella leapt effortlessly onto the RV's dinette table with a chirp, her tail flicking with importance. She pawed at the mysterious book they'd left open, nudging it until it landed on a new page —one they hadn't turned to yet.

Haylee blinked. "Okay, that's not subtle."

David chuckled under his breath. "Maybe she's your research assistant now." Riles, still rubbing sleep from his eyes, muttered, "If that cat starts talking, I'm out."

Bella only blinked slowly, then turned her back to them like the matter was settled.

Paired and Watchful

Later that morning, the group split into pairs—Haylee with Sam, David with Riles—ensuring Haylee was never left alone.

Josie bounced along with David and Riles as they swept through the forest edges. Bella, true to her feline nature, found the sink in Bertha and curled up for a nap.

David and Riles discovered more traps, some buried deep under leaves and earth. Together, they cleared the debris and reset them.

"You never know," Riles muttered. "These may come in handy."

As they worked, David spoke up. "She's changing. Haylee, I mean. She's not the same girl we started this trip with."

Riles nodded, glancing back toward the cabin. "She's not just following the trail now. She's forging it."

Meanwhile, Haylee and Sam wandered through a different part of the forest, hands brushing now and then, steps slow and thoughtful.

"What do you think Aggie has planned for you?" Sam asked, keeping his voice low.

Haylee sighed. "I don't really know. I've tried to remember those summers, but they're foggy. Like looking at stars through water. I keep getting this feeling there's something I'm supposed to find or do."

"Maybe it's not about finding," Sam said gently. "Maybe it's about becoming." Haylee looked at him, heart full. "Maybe it's both."

Tethers and Tremors

By midday, David tried to reach Ray on his phone. It went straight to voicemail. He stared at the screen, lips pressed tight.

"Still nothing?" Riles asked as he finished topping off the Jeep with fuel.

David shook his head. "No answer. But Ray can handle himself. He's probably laying low."

Riles didn't argue, but the worry in David's voice didn't go unnoticed.

They drove into town to stock up on groceries, fuel, cleaning supplies, and gear for solar-powered security lights and motion sensors—anything to help prepare the cabin for whatever came next.

Back at the site, Sam and Haylee remained at the cabin. With Bella sunning herself on the dashboard and Josie sprawled in a shady patch near the steps, it felt like the world had paused for them.

"Feels strange without them here," Haylee murmured.

"A little quiet might do us some good," Sam replied, slipping his arm around her waist.

They headed into the cabin together, unaware that beneath the silence, the forest was listening.

Fractures in the Stillness

Inside the cabin, the quiet was deceiving. Dust motes hung in shafts of sunlight like secrets suspended in time.

Haylee stared at the book they'd left earlier on the table. Her fingertips hovered over its cover but didn't touch it. "I can't stay here much longer," she said quietly.

Sam looked up from where he was organizing the supplies they had left unpacked. "What do you mean?"

"I mean here. The cabin. I know it's safe, and that there's more to learn—but my mind won't stop spinning." She paced toward the window, gazing into the trees. "It's like the walls are whispering all the time. I can't tell what's memory and what's mine."

Sam studied her, then stepped forward, gently brushing his hand along her shoulder. "You want to go."

She nodded. "Just for a little while. Just us. I need to breathe without feeling like I'm being watched—by spirits or shadows or my own thoughts."

He considered this, then smiled faintly. "Then let's go. Just tell me when."

Haylee smiled, relief washing through her. "Soon. After David and Riles get back. I just… need to feel the road again under my feet. Like I'm choosing where I go."

From the cracked window, Bella meowed softly from the RV as if she, too, agreed.

Outside, the shadows stretched longer through the trees. But inside, for the first time in days, Haylee felt a little lighter.

By the time David and Riles returned, the sun was beginning its slow descent behind the pines. The back of their Jeep was loaded with gear—solar lights, motion sensors, fuel cans, and food supplies—but their easy conversation faded when they caught sight of Bertha.

Sam was outside, tying down one of the storage bins. Haylee emerged from the RV.

Riles raised an eyebrow. "You two going somewhere?"

Sam glanced at Haylee, who nodded and stepped forward. "Just for a little while."

David frowned, his protective instincts already twitching. "Something happen?"
"No," Haylee said quickly. "Not exactly. It's just… I'm restless. I need time to think, to breathe without all the noise."

David hesitated. "The cabin is safe."

"It's not the safety," Haylee said gently. "It's me. There's something shifting—inside. The visions, the feelings, the knowing… it's like everything's coming at once and I can't hold on to who I am in the middle of it."

Riles leaned on the hood of the Jeep. "You think leaving will help?"

Haylee nodded. "I just need the road again. Just for a bit."

David looked at her—really looked—and this time, he didn't try to stop her. "You'll come back?"

"We always do," Sam said.

David and Riles climbed into Bertha and quietly gathered the last of their gear. Riles offered a two-fingered salute. "Try not to miss us too much."

David placed a hand on Haylee's shoulder. "Stay sharp. Trust yourself."

"I will," she said.

And just like that, they were off again—Haylee and Sam, back on the open road. Not running. Just moving. Searching for silence loud enough to hear the truth inside her.

Chapter Thirty-Two:
Clarity in Motion

The tires hummed against the pavement like a soft lullaby, steady and rhythmic, a sound that somehow soothed the parts of Haylee that words never could. Bertha cruised along the two-lane back road, trees rising on either side like old sentinels, their leafy arms dappling sunlight across the windshield.

Haylee sat in the driver's seat with one hand on the wheel and the other loosely gripping her coffee mug, now lukewarm. Sam was in the passenger seat, legs stretched out, sneakers propped on the dash, gazing out the window in companionable silence. Josie snored lightly at Haylee's feet, her freshly trimmed fur soft against Haylee's ankle, while Bella perched like a queen on the dashboard, tail flicking to the rhythm of the road.

No one spoke for a long while, and it was perfect.

It wasn't escape, not exactly. Haylee had stopped calling it that. It was more like shedding—a slow unraveling of the weight she carried, thought by thought, mile by mile. The deeper they went into the landscape, the quieter her mind became. The questions didn't vanish, but they softened. So did the ache.

She glanced sideways at Sam, and he gave her a half-smile like he knew. Maybe he did. Maybe he always had.

"I don't know where we're going," she said finally.

"Good," Sam replied. "That means we're getting somewhere."

The sun crept lower, casting golden streaks across the dashboard. Bertha hummed steadily along, a long stretch of asphalt that could lead anywhere—or nowhere in particular. That, strangely, was the beauty of it.

Sam shifted in his seat and turned toward her, his voice gentle.

"How're you feeling?"

Haylee didn't answer right away. She let the question hang there, watching the road snake ahead like a ribbon unraveling through the trees.

"I don't know," she said finally. "Lighter. Tired. A little like I'm coming up for air and realizing I've been underwater for a while."

Sam nodded, understanding in his silence.

"You want me to drive for a bit?" he asked. "We can pull over, switch."

She glanced at him, a soft smile playing at the edge of her lips. "Thanks, but I'm okay for now. Driving... helps me think. And not think. It's like... my body's busy so my brain can just float."

He chuckled. "Floating sounds good."

For a few moments, the only sound was the road and Josie's soft snoring. Then, Sam reached over and gently took her hand. No pressure, no expectations—just warmth, steady and sure.

Haylee looked at their hands, fingers intertwined, and squeezed his once in quiet gratitude.

"We don't have a destination, you know," she said, her voice barely above the hum of the tires. "No plan. No map. Just this."

"That's what makes it all work," Sam replied, his eyes still on the horizon. "Sometimes the best way to find something is to stop looking so damn hard."

She leaned her head back against the seat, exhaling slowly.

"Miles and miles of not looking," she murmured.

They drove on like that—hand in hand, hearts in sync, letting the open road carry them forward into the unknown.

Off the Map

They didn't plan to stop in California's desert heart—but Bertha had a way of choosing her own detours.

Somewhere past the Salton Sea, the pavement thinned and cracked like a dried-out riverbed. The sun dipped low, and a hand-painted sign appeared, nailed to a crooked post and barely legible in the dusty wind:

"Slab City →"

No Rules. No Fees. No Bullshit.

Sam raised an eyebrow. "That's… not ominous at all."

Haylee smirked. "It's perfect."

Bertha groaned slightly as she eased onto the narrow turnoff. The road twisted like it had secrets and wasn't in a rush to share them. The farther they went, the more the landscape opened into a basin scattered with mismatched architecture—old trailers sun-faded and half-sunk into the sand, painted school buses, tents stitched together with tarp and hope, makeshift gardens sprouting from bathtubs.

It wasn't a town so much as a defiant exhale. A place people arrived when they had nowhere else to be—and no intention of leaving.

A woman with long gray braids and a woven sunhat stood at the edge of a structure made of driftwood and mirrors, waving as they pulled in.

"Welcome to Slab," she called. "You'll find what you didn't know you were looking for—unless it finds you first."

Bella let out a low, curious trill on the dashboard. Josie lifted her head but didn't bark—just watched with calm eyes, as if she'd seen this kind of magic before.

Haylee looked over at Sam, her fingers tightening slightly on the wheel.

"We've officially gone off the map," she said.

Sam leaned forward, taking it all in with a grin. "Then let's see what's here."

The Woman Who Remembered

The woman with the braids stepped closer as Bertha rolled to a stop. Her sandals were made from old tires, her layered skirts fluttering in the hot wind. She looked like time had carved stories into her skin—and she wore them proudly.

Haylee opened the door, the heat wrapping around her like a thick, familiar blanket. Josie jumped down beside her, tail wagging slowly. Bella remained on the dash, gaze unblinking.

The woman's eyes flicked over Haylee briefly—polite but distant—before settling fully on Bertha. She tilted her head, lips curling into something that was not quite a smile, more like recognition.

"Well I'll be damned," she murmured, stepping closer. "Didn't think I'd ever see this girl again."

Haylee blinked. "You've seen this RV before?"

"Oh yeah," the woman said, patting the side panel like it was an old friend. "Knew the one who drove her. Wasn't her name I remembered first—it was the way she moved. Like the road bent around her instead of the other way 'round." She looked up at Haylee, a hint of mischief behind her weathered eyes. "She yours now?"

Haylee nodded slowly. "She is."

The woman studied her for a moment. "Figures."

Before Haylee could ask what that meant, the woman turned and started walking toward the driftwood-and-mirror structure she'd emerged from. "You stayin' the night?" she called over her shoulder.

Sam stepped out of Bertha, stretching. "Haylee?"

"Got space. Company's up to you. But I've got something you might want to see." She paused at her threshold and looked back at Haylee. "Something your road might be ready for."

Haylee felt a strange, weightless tug in her chest. A sense that this stop—unplanned and unscripted—was exactly where she was meant to be.

She glanced at Sam. He gave a little nod, as if to say, Go on. I'm right here.

And with that, she followed the woman off the map, into the heat-hummed shelter of memory, mirrors, and whatever came next.

Inside the shelter, the air shifted.

It wasn't cooler—if anything, it held the same heavy warmth as outside—but there was a hush to it. Like stepping into a place the desert had chosen to keep sacred. The walls were patchworks of driftwood, cracked mirrors, and sun-bleached canvases painted with spirals, eyes, and symbols Haylee couldn't quite decipher.

The woman moved with unhurried grace, weaving between piles of books, wind chimes, jars of buttons and bones, and stacks of old postcards bundled in twine. She stopped at a low shelf and pulled out a shallow tin box—worn at the corners, its label long since faded.

"She used to leave things behind," the woman said, almost to herself. "Said the road would know who needed them next."

Haylee's breath caught.

The woman opened the box with care, revealing a few odds and ends: a brass key with a feather etched into it, a tiny spiral-bound notebook stained with coffee rings, and a Polaroid of a younger version of the woman, arm slung around someone who stood just out of frame. Just enough wild hair was visible to stir something inside Haylee's memory.

The woman held up the notebook. "This one's meant for you, I think. She didn't leave it with a name. Just a knowing."

Haylee reached out, hesitant at first, then took the notebook in both hands. The cover was soft from years of being touched, but the moment it met her palms, something shifted. A subtle vibration, a flicker behind her eyes—like the feeling of remembering a dream you didn't know you had.

"She never stayed long," the woman said softly. "But she always left a mark."

Haylee looked up. "Do you remember her name?"

The woman smiled like she knew the answer—and knew better than to give it. "I remember her spirit. That's more important."

Outside, Bella meowed softly from the dash, and Josie let out a single bark like punctuation.

Sam stepped just inside the doorway, silhouetted by golden light. "Everything okay in here?"

Haylee turned to him, notebook pressed against her chest like it had always belonged there.

 "Yeah," she said. "I think... I just found something I didn't know I was looking for."

The woman nodded once, like she'd been waiting to hear those words all along.

Where We Park

Back in Bertha, the notebook sat between them like a fragile secret.

Haylee hadn't opened it yet. She wasn't ready—not just yet. For now, it rested on the console while she drove, fingers drumming absently on the wheel. Sam didn't push. He seemed to understand the way she needed to hold something close before she could unfold it.

They left Slab City behind as the sky shifted toward that dusky lavender that only deserts seem to know. Miles passed quietly, with just the hum of the engine and the occasional bark from Josie when she spotted movement outside. Bella had curled into a crescent moon on Sam's lap, completely unbothered.

About ten minutes down a dirt road that looked more like suggestion than path, they found a wide, flat patch of earth rimmed by scrub and low Joshua trees. No hookups. No fences. Just open sky and cracked earth—boondocking perfection.

"This good?" Haylee asked, already knowing the answer.

Sam nodded, grinning. "Couldn't be better."

Bertha hissed to a stop as she settled, the solar panels catching the last blush of daylight. Sam hopped out to level her while Haylee checked the inverter. Systems were all green. Power from the sun, water in the tank, freedom in every direction.

Once they were set up, Haylee climbed into the passenger seat and picked up the notebook again. It was warm, like it had absorbed the heat of everything it had ever been near.

Outside, the world was quiet. The kind of quiet that invites thoughts to rise gently, like dust in the light.

She hadn't even opened the first page, but something about holding it already made her feel less alone.

Later, after dinner and dishes were done with more laughter than effort, they spread a blanket just outside Bertha's open side door. The desert night unfolded around them, vast and full of secrets. No city lights, no other voices. Just the occasional rustle of the wind through dry brush and the far-off call of something wild.

Josie flopped down nearby with a triumphant grunt, a weathered stick proudly lodged between her paws. She chewed like it was her life's calling. Bella stretched along the edge of the blanket, her gray coat glowing in the moonlight, tail flicking contentedly.

Haylee lay back and exhaled, staring up at the sky as it deepened from lavender to indigo. The stars were sharp, as if the desert had scraped the air clean. She could see the curve of the Milky Way, a shimmer that felt both impossibly far and right above her skin.

"I don't know what this place is doing to me," Haylee whispered, eyes still on the stars.

"Maybe it's not doing anything," Sam said quietly. "Maybe it's just letting you be."

She turned to look at him. He was already looking at her, like he had been for a while. The firelight traced the line of his jaw, the curve of his mouth, the quiet behind his eyes. Something soft broke open between them—something familiar, but deeper now.

Haylee reached for his hand, and Sam met her halfway, lacing their fingers together.

He leaned in slowly, their lips met, gentle at first, like a question. Then again, a little firmer, a little surer. Her hand slid to his chest, feeling the steady thrum of his heartbeat beneath the cotton of his shirt. He pulled her in, arms wrapping around her like he'd been waiting for this moment since being on the road again.

They didn't speak. They didn't need to.

They just lay curled together under the open sky, warm against the desert night. Bella stretched and shifted, purring louder now. Josie flopped over with a happy sigh, stick abandoned.

And for one perfect, infinite night, it was just the four of them.

A woman, a guy, a dog, a cat.

And the stars.

The desert sunrise arrived like a slow inhale—soft pinks bleeding into gold, stretching long shadows across the sand. Bertha glowed warm in the early light, her windows catching the reflection of a sky that looked freshly painted.

Haylee stirred first, tucked into Sam's side beneath a woven blanket. He was still asleep, one arm loosely wrapped around her waist, his breath steady and slow. Josie had curled into a fuzzy doughnut beside them at some point in the night. Bella had claimed the warmest patch of blanket without negotiation.

Haylee didn't move for a while. She just watched the sun lift itself over the horizon, feeling—maybe for the first time in weeks—like her thoughts weren't chasing her. Like they'd finally caught up and settled beside her, content to rest too.

When Sam opened his eyes, he looked at her like he already knew what she was thinking. No words, just a soft smile that reached all the way into his gaze.

They made breakfast in that same slow rhythm—coffee brewed in the French press, leftover bread toasted on the skillet, apples sliced with a dull pocketknife. They sat on the steps of Bertha, legs brushing, watching the light shift over the landscape like it was putting on a show just for them.

No rush. No buzz. Just here. Just now.

Eventually, Haylee reached for the notebook.

It had waited through the night, quiet and patient, like it knew not to speak until the moment was right. She ran her fingers over the worn cover once more, then looked at Sam.

"Ready?" she asked softly.

He nodded. "Whenever you are."

Haylee opened to the first page.

Margins and Meaning

The first few pages were mostly sketches—swirling spirals, sunbursts, stick figures dancing beneath stars. Bits of poetry appeared between the drawings, scrawled at slants and in odd places, like the words had arrived suddenly and demanded to be written right then.

The road isn't a line.
It's a rhythm, a heartbeat.
You don't follow it—you feel it.

Haylee flipped carefully, pages soft and smudged in places, some with coffee stains or fingerprints that looked like charcoal. The notebook didn't follow a pattern. There were no dates, no chapters. Just fragments, like pieces of a dream captured before they could fade.

Sam read over her shoulder in silence.

About halfway through, Haylee's breath caught. There, tucked into the margin beside a short riddle about a key and a shadow, was a note written in a different ink—still loopy and wild, but more deliberate:

For when she's ready.
If you're reading this, it means you made it to Bertha—and beyond.
You always were meant to roam.
Trust the questions. Not the answers.
You'll know what to do when the road hums.
—A

Haylee's fingers trembled slightly as she traced the initials. She didn't say anything. Didn't need to. Sam reached over and gently brushed her knee with his hand.

Page after page followed—poems about firelight and freedom, odd little riddles that felt half nonsense and half prophecy. Haikus about wind. A shopping list with "dried mango, river rock, and trust" written underlined. A map doodled with no labels, just a tiny heart drawn somewhere in the center.

There was no explanation. No direct answers. But it felt like Aggie in every line.

Wild. Free. Unapologetically strange.

And somehow, Haylee didn't feel lost reading it. She felt... understood.

"She left this for me," Haylee said softly.

Sam nodded.

Haylee looked out the window at the wide, wild world waiting beyond their little boondocked haven.

"We have to keep going."

Chapter Thirty-Three:
Echo Reading

They had only meant to stop for gas.

Just outside Taos, in a blink-and-you-miss-it patch of adobe storefronts and rusted wind sculptures, Bertha pulled into a dusty lot next to a small café and a general store that doubled as a feed shop. Haylee stepped out to stretch, her feet crunching over gravel, when she saw it.

A faded flyer fluttered lazily on a sun-bleached telephone pole near the entrance.

"Readings by Corinne — Past. Present. Unspoken.

Walk-ins welcome. Follow the sound of the bells."

The edges were curled and weathered, but the moment Haylee laid eyes on it, a ripple passed through her—subtle, like the feeling of remembering a dream halfway through waking. That ping. The same one she felt in Aggie's hidden room, when everything she thought she knew had shifted.

She stared at the flyer, heart steady but alert.

Sam came up beside her, coffee in hand, and followed her gaze.

"You okay?" he asked.

"I think I need to go here," Haylee said quietly, almost to herself.

Sam looked at her for a long moment. In another time, he might have questioned it, might have tried to protect her from what he couldn't understand. But now, after Slab City, after the notebook, after nights under stars and truths unspooling slowly—he simply nodded.

"You have nothing to lose by going," he said. "But everything to gain."

Haylee exhaled, a mix of nerves and certainty settling into her chest.

"Yeah. I think I do."

Bella meowed softly from inside the RV window, staring toward the road like she already knew the way.

Haylee stepped closer and read the flyer again, this time aloud:

"Walk-ins welcome. Follow the sound of the bells."

It was simple, hand-lettered in ink that had bled a little in the sun, but something about it felt alive—like it had been waiting for her. She tore off the small tab at the bottom with the address and tucked it into her pocket.

They followed the directions a few blocks off the main road, winding past low stucco homes, sunflowers bending in the breeze, and a hand-carved sign that simply said **"Corinne."**

A small copper bell above the gate jingled as they stepped through. The sound echoed faintly—just once—and then the wind went still.

The front yard was wild with lavender and desert sage. Wind chimes made of antlers, crystals, and tiny spoons danced softly beneath the porch eaves. A porch swing creaked with the rhythm of the wind, but no one sat in it.

Haylee knocked once on the old turquoise door. It opened before she could knock again.

Corinne wasn't what Haylee expected. She wasn't swathed in scarves or trailing incense. She wore jeans, a white linen blouse, and a long braid streaked with gray. Her eyes were a clear, piercing amber—like someone who had seen enough to stop being surprised.

"You're right on time," Corinne said, stepping aside. "Come in."

Inside, the room was warm and welcoming—earthy wood shelves lined with books, a low table spread with a simple cloth, and a tray of loose stones and herbs. Light filtered through a stained glass window, casting soft color across the floor.

Corinne moved quietly, gracefully, as if she knew where everything was without having to look. She offered no small talk—just a gentle gesture for Haylee to sit.

"We'll start with tarot," she said, shuffling the deck with practiced ease. "Let the symbols speak first."

Haylee nodded. She glanced at Sam, who sat nearby, calm and observant but giving her space. Bella had settled at the edge of the rug like a furry guardian. Even Josie, uncharacteristically still, lay curled beside the chair.

Corinne laid out three cards.

The first: **The Moon**—mystery, illusion, the unknown.

The second: **The Fool**—new beginnings, trust, the leap.

The third: **The Tower**—revelation, upheaval, necessary change.

Corinne didn't flinch.

"You've already started your leap," she said, tapping The Fool gently. "But the path you're on? It's tied to a story that isn't finished. Someone left the door open before they were done writing."

Haylee's breath caught.

"May I?" Corinne asked, holding out her hand.

Haylee offered her palm, and Corinne traced it lightly, fingers cool and sure. "There's an energy wound here," she murmured. "Not a scar. Not yet. It's still active. Still binding you to something... or someone."

She closed her eyes for a moment, letting silence gather like breath before a storm.

"You're walking between truths," she said softly. "And not all of them belong to you."

Corinne opened her eyes again—sharper now, like she was seeing more than Haylee could.

"There's another presence," she said. "Something familiar, but veiled. I can't see him. And that's not nothing. That's... deliberate."

Haylee sat very still.

Corinne reached for a stone—rose quartz—and placed it gently in Haylee's hand. "Keep this near while you sleep. It won't answer questions, but it might help you hold them."

Then, more gently, "You already know more than you think. The knowing is just waiting for you to stop looking."

Corinne stayed quiet for a long moment, her fingers lightly touching the final tarot card—**The Tower**. She didn't speak until the silence had settled fully into the room, like a second heartbeat.

"You're standing in the rubble of someone else's choices," she said finally, eyes on Haylee. "But the house that falls isn't always the one you built—it can be the one you inherited."

Haylee's chest tightened, but she didn't look away.

"You feel like you're just now waking up to your own power," Corinne continued. "But power that's buried isn't always forgotten. Sometimes it was hidden for a reason. Not to keep you from it, but to keep others safe from what might have happened if you'd found it too soon."

Haylee swallowed hard.

Corinne reached for a small bowl beside the cards and plucked out a slip of paper folded tight. She didn't look at it before handing it to Haylee.

"It's something I wrote weeks ago. I didn't know who it was for until you walked in."

Haylee unfolded it.

"The one who watches wears two faces.
The one who waits has none.
Choose the path of echo, not shadow.
The key opens more than a door."

She read it twice.

"What does it mean?" she whispered.

Corinne leaned back. "I don't always know. I don't need to. What I do know is that you've already met both of them—the watcher and the one who waits. One has roots in your past. The other, you haven't seen clearly yet. But they've both seen you."

Haylee looked at Sam, who was watching quietly but with furrowed brows, his protective instinct barely contained.

Corinne met his eyes. "She's not in danger," she said calmly. "But she is... marked. Not cursed. Not doomed. *Marked*. As in, chosen."

Bella let out a low, almost growl-like sound from across the room. Not threatening—more like acknowledgment.

Corinne glanced toward the cat, then smiled faintly. "Your guide sees it too."

She stood and walked to a nearby shelf, pulling down a worn paperback journal. She flipped through it quickly, then tore out a single page, handing it to Haylee.

"This is a place. You'll know what to do when you get there. But don't go looking for answers. Go listening."

Haylee stared at the page. It had a rough sketch of what looked like an arch made of stone, with the words "Whisper Ridge" scribbled beneath it.

"Where is this?" she asked.

Corinne simply said, "Off the map. Like most important things."

Haylee folded the paper gently and tucked it into her journal, alongside the rose quartz. Her fingers lingered there for a second longer than necessary, grounding herself.

Corinne rose and gave a slight nod—not ceremonial, just sincere.

"Thank you," Haylee said, her voice quiet but full. "This was... more than I expected."

Corinne smiled softly. "It always is."

Sam offered a firm, respectful handshake. "You've given her a lot to think about."

Corinne held his gaze for a heartbeat longer than usual. "Stay close. Not just to her. To yourself."

Then, with a small, final gesture, she opened the door and let the sunlight flood in.

The air outside was warm and dry, the kind that seemed to press gently against your skin, like it wanted you to pay attention. As they walked back toward Bertha, the gravel crunched beneath their boots, each step slow, thoughtful.

Haylee still held the sketch of Whisper Ridge in one hand, edges flapping slightly in the breeze.

"She said I've already met both of them," she said after a while. "The one who watches, and the one who waits."

Sam nodded slowly. "I've got a guess on one of them."

Haylee glanced sideways at him.

Sam looked forward, jaw set just a little tighter than before. "I don't trust him. I don't like how his name always sits in the shadows of everything."

"Elliot," Haylee said, and the word tasted strange in the sunlight. "She couldn't see him. That's what gets me."

"Some people hide behind magic," Sam said. "Others are magic. Maybe he's both. But that doesn't mean he gets to steer this."

She stopped walking and turned to him, sunlight catching in her hair. "Thank you," she said, her voice low but sure. "For being with me. For trusting this—us. I'm more than glad you're here."

Sam looked at her, expression soft but steady. "Haylee," he said, reaching for her hand, "being with you doesn't feel like something I'm doing—it feels like who I'm becoming."

She smiled then, wide and real, and it reached all the way to her eyes. There was no doubt in her gaze, no question of whether she deserved this love. She did. And he knew it too.

He leaned in, pressing his forehead gently to hers.

229

"I fall a little more in love with you every day," he murmured. "And I'm not going anywhere."

Her breath caught—not from fear this time, but from the overwhelming beauty of being seen. Really, finally seen.

They stood like that for a moment, held together by dust and sunlight and the quiet kind of love that grows in safe places.

When they pulled apart, Haylee looked at the sketch again.

"Whisper Ridge," she said. "It sounds like something out of a dream."

Sam smiled. "Then I guess we follow the road... and listen carefully."

Together, they climbed back into Bertha, the door clicking shut with familiar comfort. Bella jumped to the dash. Josie gave a sleepy tail thump.

And the road waited—quiet, humming, ready.

The Ones Who Stayed

The hum of the drill broke the quiet.

David stood at the edge of the cabin's back porch, watching Riles mount the final solar-powered motion light to the beam just above the doorframe. The sun had already dipped behind the ridge, but the sky still held that dusky violet hue that made shadows stretch long and uncertain.

"Try it now," Riles called, stepping down from the ladder and brushing the dust off his hands.

David flipped the switch on the master panel inside. A soft click. Then a bright, focused beam of light arced across the clearing, illuminating the trees in a sweeping semicircle.

"Nice," David said, the corner of his mouth lifting.

Riles nodded, pleased. "No one's sneaking up on us now."

They had installed three of the units—one out front, one at the back, and another covering the old trail that led up from the riverbed. It was a simple setup, but effective. Enough to buy them time if someone—or something—came looking.

They stood in silence for a minute, the soft hum of the forest wrapping around them.

David pulled out his phone and checked it again. Nothing.

Riles didn't ask—he already knew the answer.

"Still no word from Ray?" he asked anyway.

David shook his head. "Not a text. Not a call. Not even a cryptic burner number."

231

"You think that's a bad sign?"

David sighed and leaned against the railing. "With Ray? Not necessarily. Could mean he's close to something. Could mean he's being watched. Or..." He didn't finish the thought.

"Or he's gone off-grid for good," Riles said for him.

David didn't respond. Just stared into the trees.

The light clicked off automatically after its cycle. Shadows crept back in.

"You think she'll find what she's looking for?" Riles asked quietly.

David rubbed a hand across the back of his neck. "I think she already has. Just doesn't know it yet."

They stayed there a while longer, letting the darkness settle around them. Not in fear. Just in awareness. The kind that comes when you've lived long enough to know that the quiet doesn't always mean peace.

Sometimes, it just means something's coming.

Later that night, David's phone buzzed.

He snatched it up before the screen could even light fully. Riles looked over from where he was rinsing out a coffee mug in the sink.

David opened the message. Short. Clean. No extra fluff.

Just checking in. We're safe. Heading toward a place called Whisper Ridge to check something out. Not sure how long we'll stay. Will keep in touch. — H.

He read it twice.

"Haylee?" Riles asked, drying his hands.

David nodded. "Yeah. They're okay. Heading somewhere called Whisper Ridge."

Riles raised an eyebrow. "That sounds... dramatic."

"Sounds like her," David said, but the relief in his voice softened the edge. He typed a quick response:

Got it. Thanks for checking in. Stay alert. You know how to reach me if you need anything. —D

He hovered for a second, then added:
Proud of you.

Then he hit send.

Riles leaned against the counter. "Think she told us everything?"

David shook his head, just once. "No. But she told us enough."

They stood there in silence for a beat, the hum of the security system softly ticking beneath it.

"She's trusting her instincts," David added. "I think... for the first time in a long time."

Riles nodded. "About time someone did."

David glanced out the window, where the last motion light blinked on, casting a pool of light across the trail.

"She'll find what she's looking for," he said. "Or it'll find her."

Chapter Thirty-Four:
The Ridge Knows

It started with Bella.

She had been calm most of the drive, nestled in the curve of the dashboard as Bertha rolled along the winding New Mexico backroads. But as they got closer to the coordinates scribbled beneath Whisper Ridge, her tail began to twitch—not lazily, but sharply. Her ears flicked toward sounds Haylee couldn't hear, and her pupils stayed wide, even in daylight.

Sam noticed first.

"Your girl's spooked," he said, eyeing the cat as she rose onto all fours and stared out the windshield, alert and silent.

"She's not scared," Haylee murmured, her hands tight on the wheel. "She's sensing something. Something... big."

Haylee had been feeling it too—not like the soft, intuitive pings she was used to, but something heavier. Sharper. It was like standing barefoot on the edge of a live wire. Her skin buzzed. The air felt too thin, too still. Even Bertha's engine sounded muffled, like the world was holding its breath.

Josie let out a low whine in the back and curled herself into a tighter ball, ears flicking.

Sam leaned forward in his seat. "This is it?"

Haylee nodded. "It's close."

The road had narrowed to a single lane, cutting through a canyon wall with no signs, no fences, no hint of what was coming. But she could feel it—like the land was pressing against her, testing her.

The GPS signal cut out two minutes before the pin was supposed to drop. No reception. Just open sky and silence.

Bella jumped down and padded to the back of the RV, sitting near the door like she was waiting for something—or someone—to open it.

Sam looked at Haylee.

"Still sure?"

She didn't hesitate. "More than ever."

Bertha climbed the final incline, her wheels crunching over dry gravel. And then the ridge appeared—quiet, weathered, ancient in a way that had nothing to do with time.

A stone arch stood at the base of the trailhead. The same one Corinne had drawn. No markings. No signs. Just the shape, unmistakable.

Haylee parked and killed the engine.

Everything went quiet.

Not the kind of quiet that brings peace. The kind that makes you feel like you're being watched.

Haylee stepped out of Bertha and immediately felt the shift.

It wasn't just the dry air or the altitude. It was something underneath all that—a hum beneath the soles of her boots, like the ground itself was alive with memory. The kind of feeling you don't name. You just feel.

Sam joined her on the passenger side, eyes scanning the landscape. It was beautiful in a stark, almost brutal way—sun-bleached stone, scrub brush clinging to life, sky stretched wide and unbroken. But it didn't feel empty.

It felt... crowded with silence.

Josie padded out behind them, tail low, ears swiveling back. She let out a soft, uneasy whine and pressed gently against Haylee's leg—not in fear, but in instinct. She'd go, but she didn't like it.

Then Bella darted out of Bertha like a gray arrow across the dirt, sprinting toward the ridge—and stopping just shy of the stone arch. She turned and sat, staring at them over her shoulder, as if to say, Well? You coming or not?

"She knows," Haylee whispered.

Sam nodded slowly. "They both do."

He took a step forward, then turned to her. "You okay?"

"I don't think this place *wants* us to be okay," Haylee said, staring up at the ridge. "But I think it wants us to *know*."

He stepped beside her, close but not crowding. "This doesn't feel like just a location," he said. "It feels like..."

"A threshold," she finished for him. "It feels like a line."

They stood there together, the wind shifting softly around them, lifting strands of Haylee's hair and stirring dust into faint spirals at their feet. The air held weight—like the echo of something waiting to be named.

Bella stood and walked slowly beneath the arch, then stopped again, turning her head just enough to keep them in her gaze.

"She's leading us," Haylee said.

Sam offered his hand. "Then let's follow."

Together, they stepped beneath the arch.

And the ridge welcomed them.

The trail curved upward, narrow and uneven, forcing them to walk single file. Bella led the way without hesitation—tail high, pausing only to glance back, her pale fur flickering like a phantom against the sunbaked stone.

The higher they climbed, the quieter everything became.

No birdsong. No wind. Even their footsteps seemed muffled, as if the ground had decided sound no longer belonged here.

"Feels like we're walking into a memory," Sam murmured.

Haylee didn't answer. She couldn't. Her whole body buzzed—not with fear, but anticipation. Every instinct she had, every flicker of intuition, every whisper of magic she didn't fully understand yet—it was *screaming now*. Not in warning. In recognition.

She had been here before. Not physically. But somewhere deeper.
The path opened suddenly into a wide plateau framed by curved rock formations. In the center sat what looked like a **low stone structure**, circular and half-sunk into the ground. Not a ruin. Not a home.

It looked like a place meant for *remembering*.

Haylee slowed, her breath catching. "This is it."

Bella circled the structure once, then leapt lightly onto the flat top of a nearby boulder and sat, tail flicking, eyes fixed on Haylee.

There were symbols carved into the stone—some faded, some sharp. Spirals, keys, a single crescent. Haylee ran her fingers across one without realizing it, and the second she did—

everything shifted.

Not the earth. Not the sky. Something within her.

A flash of light—not blinding, but internal. Images surged in her mind: a woman's silhouette in a storm, a figure watching from across a field of dust, and the sound—clear as a bell—of someone calling her name.

But not aloud.

Inside.

"Haylee?"

Sam's voice brought her back. She blinked. Her hand was still on the stone. "I saw something," she said. "Felt something. Like I was being pulled into something old."

Sam knelt beside her. "Is it safe?"

"No," she said softly. "But I think it's *true.*"

Just then, Bella stood—her back arched, fur bristling—and hissed sharply toward the edge of the ridge. Josie growled low and got between Haylee and the drop-off.

Haylee and Sam both turned.

A figure stood across the stone, just beyond the ridge's edge. Too far to see clearly. Still. Watching.

Not approaching.

Just there.

And then—

gone.

Not vanished in motion. Just... no longer part of the world in front of them. Sam rose instantly, eyes sharp. "Did you see that?"

Haylee stood slowly, her voice steady despite the pounding in her chest. "Yes."

She turned back to the carved symbol—the spiral and the key—and knelt once more. Her fingers hovered, trembling now, not from fear but certainty. She reached out—

And the stone beneath her hand glowed.

A single phrase burned through her mind, not in her voice.

You are almost ready.

Then the light vanished.

The wind returned.

And in the distance, something echoed—not a sound, but a presence.

Watching.

Waiting.

About the Author

Kimber Guise is the author of Keys to Wonderlust, a story inspired by her own nomadic lifestyle. She is a full-time traveler, adventurer, and storyteller who explores the open roads of North America in her beloved RV. Accompanied by her loyal pup and curious cats, she embraces a nomadic lifestyle rich with discovery, quiet moments, and scenic detours. From winding mountain passes to tucked-away campgrounds, Kimber finds inspiration in the natural beauty of National and State Parks across the United States and Canada.

A published author and lifelong reader, Kimber believes stories have the power to connect us, heal us, and remind us who we are. When she's not writing, you'll find her chasing sunsets, sipping coffee by a campfire, or browsing the shelves of a local bookstore. She's committed to savoring the journey—wherever the road may lead.

Follow Kimber's adventures and writing life on TikTok and Instagram **@vibing.rvlife**, on Facebook at **Vibing RV Life**, or on YouTube under **Kimber Guise (@vibing.rvlife)**.

www.ingramcontent.com/pod-product-compliance
Lightning Source LLC
Chambersburg PA
CBHW051337020726
47501CB00007B/2139